The Wi

'*The Wilderness* is essentially
passions, frustrated ambitior
the hands of O'Flaherty it b
tears through the mind with the careless abandon of an Atlantic breaker.'

Sunday Press

The Black Soul

'Embodies an energy that is genius.'

W B Yeats

'An elemental book because the primitive passions run free.'

AE

Famine

'A major achievement – a masterpiece. The kind of truth only a major writer of fiction is capable of portraying.'

Anthony Burgess

'The author's skill as a storyteller is at times breathtaking. This is a most rewarding novel.'

Publishers Weekly

'A marvellously visual writer who prints his description on the retina.'

The Guardian

Skerrett

'One of the most powerful novels that this master-writer has ever produced.'

Irish Times

'Liam O'Flaherty is a great, great writer whose work must be unique in any language, any culture. He has all the potential for becoming a matrix for the yearnings of another generation.'

Neil Jordan

'Powerful in language, majestic in scope, utterly honest.'

Sunday Press

Other books by LIAM O'FLAHERTY
available from WOLFHOUND PRESS

FICTION

Famine

Short Stories: The Pedlar's Revenge

The Wilderness

Skerrett

Insurrection

The Assassin

Mr. Gilhooley

The Ecstasy of Angus

AUTOBIOGRAPHY

Shame the Devil

FOR CHILDREN

The Test of Courage

All Things Come of Age

FORTHCOMING

The Letters of Liam O'Flaherty

(Edited by A. A. Kelly)

LIAM O'FLAHERTY

Born in 1896 on Inishmore, the largest of the Aran Islands, Liam O'Flaherty grew up in a world of awesome beauty, echoes from his descendants and the ancient pagan past. From his father, a Fenian, O'Flaherty inherited a rebellious streak; from his mother, a noted *seanchaí* (storyteller), came the deep spiritualism and love of nature that has enraptured readers through the decades.

In France in 1917 O'Flaherty was severely shell-shocked. After a short recuperation, he spent several restless years travelling the globe. In 1920 he supported the Republican cause against the Free State government. Influenced by the Industrial Workers of the World's programme of social revolution, O'Flaherty organised the seizure and occupation of the Rotunda Theatre at the top of Dublin's O'Connell Street in 1922. He hoisted the red flag of revolution, calling himself the 'Chairman of the Council of the Unemployed', but fled three days later to avoid bloodshed. Later that year he moved to London, where his writing skills came to the attention of critic Edward Garnett, who recommended to Jonathan Cape the publication of O'Flaherty's first novel. For the next two decades, O'Flaherty's creative output was astonishing. Writing in English and Irish, he produced novels, memoirs and short stories by the dozen. Remarkable for their literary value and entertainment, O'Flaherty's books are also crucial from an anthropological point of view, charting the ways and beliefs of a peasant world before it was eclipsed by modernity.

Some of O'Flaherty's work was banned in Ireland – he was a rebel in his writing, as in his life. Liam O'Flaherty died in Dublin in 1984, aged 88 years, having enriched forever Irish literature and culture.

LIAM O'FLAHERTY

the wilderness

WOLFHOUND PRESS

This edition published 1996
First published 1978 by
WOLFHOUND PRESS Ltd
68 Mountjoy Square
Dublin 1

and Wolfhound Press (UK)
18 Coleswood Rd
Harpenden
Herts AL5 1EQ

First Paberback edition 1978, reprinted 1986

Wolfhound Press receives financial assistance from the Arts Council/
An Chomhairle Ealaíonn, Dublin.

British Library Cataloguing in Publication Data
A catalogue record for this book is available from the British Library.

ISBN 0 86327 534 6

The text for this edition has been edited for publication by Dr A A Kelly with the author. The original manuscript draft of the work is at the Humanities Research Centre of Texas at Austin. The only published version appeared in *The Humanist* (journal of the British Humane Society) in 1927 in serial form.

Typesetting: Wolfhound Press
Cover illustration and design: Jon Berkeley
Printed in the UK by Cox & Wyman Ltd., Reading, Berkshire.

CHAPTER I

In all our lovely land there is no valley fairer than the Fairy Glen. Deep, deep, like a hollow bowl, it lies among the mountains, so high above the plains and the sea that no man ever saw it but from the mountain tops or sailing the sky in ships. The mountains rise on every side about it; sheer sides and sloping sides and outstanding craggy heights crowned with snow. One mountain has a pointed head standing at the valley's end. And opposite, there is a recumbent, shapeless, massive mound, in whose bosom lies a dark, silent lake beneath a yellow precipice. Along the valley's sides the bare mountains are furred with pine trees. Here and there the pine trees stand on the tall horizons near the clouds, stooping forward like long men marching under heavy loads.

A river flows across the glen from the black lake, down past the pointed mountain to the plain beyond. Long ago it was called the Fairy River: at a time when the world was rich in gods, and this glen was supposed by man's imagination to be the dwelling place of gods and their attendant hosts of fairies. Now people call it the Black River. But the glen dwellers still plant rowan trees about their houses to protect them from the fairy hosts of the dead, forgotten gods.

It was a summer morning just before sunrise in this Fairy Glen. In the dawn-light the great blue roof of the sky, bright with fading stars and the coming sunlight, seemed so near that a man might reach it with his outstretched hand and pluck a star from it, just over the steep mountain sides. Down in the glen everything was dark and silent. There was no wind. The birds had not yet begun to sing. The strange bog beasts that cry at night were still. The murmur of the river water was the only sound.

The sound of the river water was majestic, awe-inspiring music. So low, so gentle, its sweet rhythm carried by the mountain echoes to the sky, its song was like the song of ghosts that move through the unknown void. The nimble water tumbled over brown, smooth rocks from the black lake among the highland crags, down the winding narrow seam in the hollowed land, through the great oak wood of the birds, past the pointed mountain to the plain beyond, singing its lovely song unceasingly. It roared through the rocky gorges, and its black water turned into white fountains and then dropped into deep pools. It rumbled smoothly, swirling over a bed of yellow sand between low banks dotted with willow trees. And its many sounds mingled, rising in harmony, a slumbrous, lapping, tingling sound, merry and mysterious.

Suddenly a bird chirped and stopped and chirped again. There was a loud shrill cry and a brown bird rose from a marsh and wheeled into the air. Rising higher and higher it cried aloud its piercing cry and disappeared over a mountain top. Then a multitude of little birds began to chirp sleepily. Soon the glen was wild with the laughter of birds, and the sun, as if it had awaited their voices, burst over a high crag to the east and lighted up a stretch of yellow-flowered gorse. As a man awaking from a formless dream seeks with his wondering eyes the dim shapes in his room, so the rays of the rising sun sped round the glen, unveiling its many beauties. The dark shapes became bright. Trees, flowers, plants, stones, grassy fields, river water and bog pools, showed their gay colours and their surface wet with dew. The night mists rose into the sky and trailing up the mountain sides they looked like long, winding shrouds covering phantom figures in flight. The belt of blue stones around the summit of the pointed mountain shone bright like a jewel above the cincture of whitish mist.

The beauty of the valley was the austere beauty of a wilderness. In spite of the gay chatter of the birds, the majesty of the mountains, the perfumed air of the summer dawn, the murmur of the river water, the great multitude of colours on the earth's surface, the beauty of the valley was sombre and austere. It had the mystery of a hidden wilderness, where men are few and the solitude makes living things brood awfully upon the majesty of the unknown universe.

There were stray houses scattered at intervals, each house surrounded by trees to protect it from the storms of winter. Their shapes looked uncouth; the clumsy work of man destroying the continuity of nature.

Just in the centre of the glen near the river there was a red-roofed house in a grove of orange-berried rowan trees. It was built on a flat field beside a little stream. There was a fence of round granite stones around it, with a black wooden gate in the fence between two hawthorn bushes, whose outer branches tipped, making a feathery arch of white blossoms. In the oblong enclosure within the fence there were three spaces: one, a grass plot in which there were fruit bushes bearing currants and gooseberries; the second, directly in front of the house, had been paved with cobble stones and laid out at intervals with flower beds that lined the walls of the house and of the fence; the third, at the far side of the house, was a thick grove of trees. But the flower beds had run wild. Grass was growing over the cobble stones. The plot of groupd in which the fruit trees grew was crowded with tall nettles. The fruit trees were stripped bare by birds. The bark of the trees and the twigs of the fruit bushes had been eaten by goats. The sheds to the right of the house were falling in ruins. The fence was unkempt. The house itself was weatherbeaten. It was a long low cottage of four rooms, with a zinc roof painted red. The four windows and the door were painted green. The walls had been whitewashed, but they were now becoming yellow. Along the front wall, where rose trees had been trained to climb, there were now bare branches clinging, fastened with nails and bits of string. While at the base of the walls, in the flower beds, nettles and other rank weeds grew among chrysanthemum shoots.

In this wild place that had once been a peasant dwellinghouse there was no sign of human life. Wild nature was quickly transforming it into the image of her own naked beauty. The black gate with its archway of white blossoms was becoming the entrance to a nettled ruin, another fairy hiding-place.

For a long time after dawn birds occupied this loneliness, singing. The bleating of goats was heard. Then came the patter of goats' feet on the zinc roof of the shed to the right of the house. Two goats appeared; one bald, one with a single horn; large brown goats with handsome udders. They slowly marched along the roof to its eastern edge and stood, staring motionless at the advancing sun, which now appeared in its full golden circumference hoisted in the blue sky above the mountain tops.

For a while they stared at the sun, with unblinking, yellow eyes, in which there was a curious melancholy wonder: the everlasting wonder of life, confronted with the beauty of the brilliant star that brings light after darkness. Their eyes wandered sharply hither and thither, and they stood closer together, as if afraid of all the world, with its host of moving, living things; striving incessantly towards an unknown goal in fear and haste;

the miracle and the mystery, which neither man nor beast can fathom.

Then the hornless one snorted. And the unicorn uttered a long melancholy cry, twisting her head aloft. They both bleated, one after the other, calling something. Then they listened with rigid ears. And hearing nothing in answer to their call, they turned about and strutted off the roof, down a broken wall into the yard. There they began to bleat more loudly, walking along the front of the house, surveying the windows, until at last there was a sound within. Both goats paused in their bleating and waited. The door opened and a man appeared.

He was a tall sinewy man of slender build, with the stern holy face of one who broods a lot in solitude. Standing in the doorway he smiled with pleasure on the goats. As he smiled, his pale, handsome face bore the ecstatic tender look of one whose being is in harmony with nature. His gentle, blue eyes, half-closed, gleamed with a fine intelligence. When a man smiles without the presence of another human being to see his face, his character is disclosed in his features. The soul appears through the eyes, as when a lover gazes at his beloved in the first joy of mating. His face was the face of a visionary, with the expression that the great artist El Greco has given to the face of Saint Francis, an expression of great suffering and great joy, as from the realisation of a love that cannot be satisfied. The features were nervous and refined. His pale skin was pure from asceticism. His whole countenance shone with spiritual beauty. His brown hair was cropped close around his skull, but on top it curled luxuriantly.

He was dressed in white pyjamas and on his bare feet he wore white canvas shoes. In his right hand he carried a bath towel.

Stepping out into the yard he called to his goats. They bleated in answer. The unicorned one came up slowly and offered her forehead to be scratched. He rubbed their foreheads and called them by their names. Then they followed him out through the gate to the little stream where he took his morning bath.

The stream was just outside the gate, along the base of the steep mountain that rose immediately beyond it. A rough track wound up the side of the mountain for a distance of half a mile to the narrow road that ran along the side of the glen, travelling across the high shoulders of the mountains. The track ran among granite boulders and clumps of gorse and through a green field that had once been tilled. Passing the front of the house, between the gate and the stream, there was another track, along which the glen dwellers passed with their carts, between the two farms on either side. These two farmsteads were visible at a distance, surrounded by trees.

The man stripped himself beside the stream, put his clothes on a rock and then bathed in a pool, while the goats stood by watching him. Then he left the water, winding his towel about his bare loins as he stepped on to a large boulder in the middle of the stream, followed by the goats. Then he stretched his hands above his head, facing the sun. The goats stood in front of him, side by side, motionless, looking sideways curiously and listening.

Already the air was warm. The sun's rays shone on his bare body, each invisible shaft of light pouring invisible fire into his blood. And from this invisible fire joy emerged, gladdening him, awakening his being to the beauty of the morning. Then a pleasant torpor overcame him, and he became motionless and at peace, listening.

Nothing moved. The goats began to chew their cud. Birds called to one another. A grasshopper, standing on the boulder, rubbed its queer wings against its thighs, making a rasping sound. Then it waited, listening. Three horses, grazing on the marshland, paused in their grazing and approached the rock, sniffing the air. Then they stood still listening. A flock of sheep moving among the gorse began to bleat. They also stood and listened. Again the music of the river water murmured its continuous song, unrivalled in the stillness. Gently, gently, the water whispered to the sun.

The wild flowers had opened their petals, passionately striving towards the light. Smoke began to rise from the scattered houses. Everything was awake. Everything listened. Everything looked upwards at the unknown emptiness with its many wonders, where the sunlight made fairy shapes among the clouds.

The man shuddered and covered his face with his hands. Then he looked about him at the listening, silent animals, and then upwards at the sky. He murmured: 'Can all this beauty have no meaning? Is all this a mirage of my imagination? Or am I really about to discover the object of life? The immortality where death and fear are unknown?'

Bees began to drone among the flowers and a sparrow hawk arose from a pine wood with a shrill cry. The man shuddered again. 'Not yet. I am still afraid. Afraid of this mystery, these beasts, birds and insects that listen and fear with me. I must become more joyous than the birds that sing to the sun because they fear the darkness. I must transcend all fear and love all things. Then all things shall be made manifest.'

He called his goats and descended from the rock.

CHAPTER II

Beneath his house on the mountainside across the river, an old man, called Patrick Macanasa, had been watching the scene on the rock. He was leaning against a low stone fence, shielding his eyes with his hands, looking intently downwards at the young man who stood on the rock beyond the red-roofed house. His old face was yellow and wrinkled. It bore the strange expression of melancholy wisdom that old ravens have. His deeply hidden grey eyes were sharp, mysterious and birdlike. His slender frame was furrowed and twisted with old age and the labour of the fields, so that his grey beard sank into his hollow neck. There were deep cavities in his cheeks, and his hands were knotted like old roots. And yet his lean body was vigorous and hard, like a slender mountain ash that bends and sways before the storm and yet does not fall. His ragged garments were patched with cloth of many colours. The colours had mingled with old age and become the colour of the ground about him, making him almost invisible against the background of the mountainside. A subtle, mysterious figure of a man.

He carried his old coat on his arm, and in his left hand he held a little stick on which he leaned as he watched. His underlip protruded, and his eyes, staring from beneath his bushy grey eyebrows, had a look of intense malice in them. For this stranger had come into his glen and taken land that had belonged to his forefathers.

Terrible and enduring is the hatred of a dying caste. Like a grass worm, it fattens on the lifeblood of each decaying limb until it reaches the last root and becomes bloated with the poison of fanaticism. This unseemly peasant was the descendant of Gaelic lords who had conquered the glen and enslaved its inhabitants: so long ago that their names, their exploits and their very gods are quite forgotten. In the glen there are relics of the Druids, where the hawthorn bushes grow in a circle around a cairn of smooth stones. There are green mounds by the river where their kings were buried. There are dim tracks among the ferns that once were chariot roads. On flat stones there are strange signs engraven which nobody can read, and which the illiterate glen dwellers hold in superstitious fear. These Gaelic lords have become fairy phantoms. Their habitations are a wilderness and their descendant a ragged knave, in whose soul their fiery lust of conquest has become degenerated into a cunning and servile avarice.

For four hundred years the Macanasas had been dispossessed of their glen by fresh conquerors, and still they believed that the glen was theirs, and that some day their inheritance would be restored to them. Despising labour, they became predatory vagabonds, seeking to gain by theft and treachery the tribute which they once took by law. The shrewd wisdom, by which aristocrats hold their serfs in bondage, had become perverted to a cunning power of flattery. And the pride of the conqueror had become an intense hatred of humanity. As their fathers built so they wished to destroy, longing to turn the glen into a manless wilderness.

Although the glen is ten miles long and two miles wide, there are now no more than fifty little houses in it. There are no villages, no shops, and each house stands remote from its fellows. Before the great famine there were many villages and the glen was merry in the evening with the laughter of young lovers courting on the roadsides in the moonlight. Then in their last mountain refuges our persecuted people were pursued by famine, which almost entirely destroyed them. The glen is thickly strewn with the ruins of their houses. And on the mountainside the fields they cultivated have again sunk back into the wilderness, overgrown with ferns and briars, with only the earthen mounds of their fences left to show that they once were tilled.

Lately, however, since the last insurrection, new people have begun to come into the glen. The newcomers belong to the city and they are intellectuals, seeking the solitude of the wild glen to think in peace. Macanasa and his four sons, who prowl about the glen as if protecting it from invasion, visited each to discover politely the cause of their coming. But as they did not purchase land they were treated with courtesy. They all occupied cottages bought from peasants who had emigrated, along the narrow high road running across the mountainsides above the glen on the western side, from the black lake to the pointed mountain. One was a scientist. Two were painters. And the other was a middle-aged maiden, a member of a landowning family that had in its turn been dispossessed in the recent insurrection. They all lived in absolute retirement from civilisation and from one another, except the maiden lady, who was reputed to be a member of some new English religious sect. She associated with the people for the purpose of learning what they knew about spirits, fairies and ogres. The

Macanasas preyed on them all, taking what they could in return for odd jobs of light work and food.

Then the young man came to the red-roofed house across the river a month ago, having purchased the house and forty acres of land at a public auction. It was this that made the old man's eyes gleam with malice. He had expected to obtain the farm for one of his sons.

The house and farm had been occupied by an old woman called Bridget Macanasa, a distant relative of Patrick's and another dying shoot of the family. She had fallen into debt, principally owing to the defalcations of her cousin, in whose hands she had placed her affairs. On her death her property was seized for debt. Another peasant called Deegan offered to buy the place, but Macanasa's family made violent threats and Deegan lost courage. The place remained unoccupied for a year, as the new owner, a shopkeeper from the little town in the plain below, could not get anyone to buy it. No farmer wanted to leave the plain and come to the glen. No glen dweller dared buy the land through fear of the Macanasas, since land grabbing, as it is called, is still a more heinous crime than murder in our country. Of course the Macanasas had positively no claim to it, other than the obscure claims of agelong tradition. But among a conquered people, traditions are more sacred than the current laws of the conquerors.

Finally the shopkeeper, as a last resort, put up the property for sale by public auction. Macanasa and his four sons attended, each carrying a heavy stick to intimidate purchasers. There were only two bidders. A wandering Jew purchased some old furniture and departed with it under police protection. The other bidder who gave his name as Henry Lawless, purchased the house and land for two hundred pounds. The Macanasas, amazed at the man's temerity, went home muttering. And two days later, Lawless arrived to take possession, accompanied by two tame goats.

Then the Macanasas began their sinister attacks. First they allowed their horses and their sheep to stray upon the stranger's land by night. As he paid no heed, they themselves moved about the land, hovering at a distance watching him. Through fear of them, nobody spoke to him. But Lawless did not seem irritated by this boycott. They noticed him acting strangely, standing on rocks and making gestures, as if in prayer, always accompanied by his goats. Old Macanasa made inquiries in the little town, but he could learn nothing about the man. So that he had at last determined to visit him.

He spat on his stick and began to walk down the mountainside towards the river. He walked as actively as a young man, in spite of his seventy years, looking around him eagerly and murmuring. Suddenly he halted on a grassy mound and took off his tattered hat. He looked all round the glen slowly and then upwards at the sky.

'Glory, glory to the great God of Heaven,' he said fervently.

His queer old face became illuminated with joy, at the glory of the morning and the beauty of the ancient glen. He leaned again on his stick, scratched his chest slowly and lowered his eyes to the ground.

Now there was no malice in his eyes, but that expression of childish awe which the eyes of old men hold when they contemplate something that they love. A peasant's love for the land is fanatical because it is his only love. His children, his wife, even his own life, are simply dear to him in relation to the soil, for whose benefit alone they are used and squandered freely. It is a lust without the emotion of passion. It is cold because it lies so deep, deep in his nature that even when a manifestation of it reaches his consciousness it comes with a dull flicker of pure joy that almost immediately is overcome with fear and perishes in a brooding hatred of something unknown. He is happy only when he is rooting the earth or tending his flocks. While resting in apparent idleness, his dull mind ponders on the growth of herds and crops and the movements of their enemies, blight, storms, rain or drought. Removed from the land, unless it be done in early youth, the peasant either becomes a degenerate profligate or withers away like a plant without sap. And in decrepit old age he clings year after year to his existence, in spite of the insults and contumlies of his children, whose avarice desires his death. Just one glimpse of the sowers on a sunny morning in spring brings greater joy to him than the victories of kings.

The old man mused, motionless, without thought, wrapt in the contemplation of the earth about him, as if listening to the throbbing of its being. Standing thus, he heard no sound of life but the noiseless presence of the earth. For a few moments he experienced an exalted happiness, and then he stood erect sharply, glanced towards the red-roofed house and moved forward hurriedly, his eyes gleaming again with malice.

He crossed the river by a narrow wooden bridge that swayed beneath his weight. The mountain began to grow right above the river bank. Descending, his feet had shuffled. Ascending now, his lean thighs were taut, and he passed along with a slow rhythmic gait, almost moving on his toes, with drooping shoulders: the gait of the mountaineer.

Presently he reached the old chariot road that wound across the valley. It was now overgrown with grass, but still used by the glen dwellers to cross the river with their carts at the ford below the bridge. There was a straight path leading directly to the rear of the house, but the old man chose to go around by the old road, in order to reach the house from the front, as a matter of courtesy. He also wanted to observe as much as possible the stranger's actions before speaking to him. However, when he debouched into the wide, long marshland in front of the house, the stranger was nowhere to be seen. The old man paused and then sat down on a rock to wait for his appearance.

His own horses, grazing at a distance, noticed him. One of them neighed, and they all simultaneously raised their tails and set off in headlong flight away from him up the mountainside. They were afraid that he came to harness them and make them work. He looked after them muttering curses. But after a few moments his eyes grew soft with pleasure, looking at the movement of their galloping limbs, the sheen of their glossy flanks in the morning sunlight and their undulating manes. The three half-wild horses, galloping unhaltered through the marshland, aroused some ancient memories in him and made his old blood throb feverishly. Just for a moment. Then his eyes grew cold. He looked towards the house again.

Still there was nothing to be seen or heard but the sleepy warblings of the birds, the droning of bees, the murmur of insects and the scarcely perceptible breathing of plants, herbs, trees, and wild flowers, that becomes a distinct, drowsy sound on a silent summer day. Restless, he got to his feet. He walked along the grassy path towards the gate. Though apprehensive, he began to feel a curious longing to approach the man within the enclosure of the house, so that he halted again and listened. He could see nothing through the thick feathery curtain of leaves that surrounded the house, and yet he felt a mysterious presence within it.

Then he reached the black gate, stopped with a gesture of terror, which was partly feigned, took off his hat and crossed himself. 'Glory be to God,' he said in a loud voice, 'ye took a start out of me.'

Lawless was sitting on a stool in the yard in front of the house having his breakfast. He was dressed in grey flannel trousers and a white shirt that was open at his throat. A leather belt encircled his waist. He still wore the white canvas shoes, without socks. The goats, which he had just milked, were lying near chewing their cud. When they saw the old man at the gate, they raised their heads nervously and thrust their ears forward. Lawless was breakfasting on their milk and a small oaten cake. The large brown pitcher of milk stood on the ground beside him. When he saw Macanasa his face clouded for a moment and then he smiled and said:

'Good-morning. Did I terrify you? Forgive me.'

When the goats heard his voice they dropped their ears, lowered their heads and began to chew their cud once more. Macanasa put on his hat and opened the gate slowly. Then he advanced hurriedly across the yard, stooping forward, with his right hand to his ear in a listening attitude. He came to Lawless's side, and holding his hand to his mouth, he said in a loud voice: 'I beg yer pardon, but I'm very deaf this twenty years. It's rheumatism.' Then he added in a lower voice, looking intently into Lawless's face: 'What's that ye said to me?'

'I asked you to forgive me for terrifying you,' said Lawless.

The old man jerked himself erect with great force and smiled, showing his yellow teeth. Then he shrugged and, shifting his stick to his right hand, he put his left hand on Lawless's shoulder and gripped the shoulder. He peered into Lawless's face closely and remained in that attitude for several moments in silence, with his eyes screwed together.

Lawless returned his stare calmly, with a remote, gentle, expression in his eyes.

'Ha,' said the old man at length. He stood erect and spat vigorously. 'God bless ye. Ye have a fine face. Ye have a fine, elegant, countenance. There's no harm in yer countenance.'

Lawless started. He blinked, furrowed his forehead, opened his lips to speak, and then, without saying anything, he glanced aside. He looked back at Macanasa and said, seriously:

'What do you see in my face?'

'I see nothing but what is good,' said Macanasa in a loud, earnest voice. He enunciated every word fiercely, like a tramp that wishes to flatter a prospective patron.

'I am glad,' said Lawless, looking at the ground. 'You are very kind. Do you live in this glen?'

'Eh? What's that ye say?' Macanasa put his hand to his ear and lowered his head.

'Do you live in this glen?' repeated Lawless. 'Are you a neighbour of mine?'

'Sure, don't I live across the river there from ye. I'm Paddy Macanasa. D'ye mean to tell me ye haven't seen me before? Or heard of me? Eh? That ye don't know me yet and ye here a month?'

Lawless looked at him calmly and shook his head.

'Your face is familiar to me,' he said, 'but then all faces are familiar to me. I don't know you more than I know other men.'

The old man stepped back and puckered up his lips in meditation. 'The man is queer in his head,' he thought. He leaned both hands on his stick, thrust out his right leg, and said: 'You mustn't take it unkindly of us to leave ye be yerself all this month without making neighbourly visits to ye and giving ye a hand in whatever way we could oblige ye. D'ye see? But we thought ye were an emergency man or maybe a detective sent to watch the people by the Government.'

Lawless looked at him in surprise. Then he got to his feet, stared again, and said: 'Won't you come into my house?' He picked up his pitcher of milk and went towards the door, followed by Macanasa.

Macanasa had been intimate with the interior of the house in the old days, and he was surprised at the change that had been wrought in it. Standing within the door, he could see three rooms, as the doors leading off the kitchen, in which he stood, into the two bedrooms were wide open. This room had formerly been a kitchen and living room in Bridget Macanasa's time. It had been a cheerful room, neatly furnished, with a dresser laden with delf, a great fire always burning on the open hearth, a table, chairs, pictures and ornaments on the walls and a spinning wheel in the corner opposite the door. Now it was absolutely devoid of furniture, excepting a large circular rush mat that lay on the cement floor. In the room to the left Macanasa saw the walls lined with books, but there was no other furniture. In the room to the right he saw a camp bedstead with a horse blanket folded at the end. There was another room opening off the bedroom to the left. There Lawless kept his trunk and food and necessary utensils. Its door was shut. The windows were bare and yet the sunlight did not penetrate very far into the house on account of the surrounding awning of trees. The silence was intense.

Lawless placed the pitcher and the loaf of bread on the window-sill and turned to Macanasa. But he suddenly remembered that there was no seat to offer the old man. He rushed out into the yard and brought in the stool. During the few moments he was absent, the old man darted to the door of the room to the left. At the far end he saw a small round table, on which rested a human skull, white and devoid of flesh. Beside the skull there was a tiny votive lamp, and on the wall, at the rear, there was a dark oil painting in a black frame. In the momentary glimpse he caught of it, the old man saw an extraordinary face in an agony of extreme pain. Terrified, he jumped back just as Lawless entered with the stool.

'Take this seat, will you?' said Lawless, placing the stool on the mat.

Macanasa sat down. He now felt nervous and cowed. When he interviewed the landowner in the old days, he always felt at his ease, in spite of the magnificent mansion, the lacqueys and the lord's power over him. For the landlord treated him as a worm, as a conquered serf. And a conquered peasant always despises those that hate him and have conquered him, even when he grovels before them. So Macanasa had despised his landlord as an inferior, whose stupid brain he was able to over-reach with his guile. He despised him as a low usurper, a fat degenerate weakling, who could not even ride a horse properly. And in the same manner, when brought before a magistrate on a charge of sheep-stealing or of intimidation or of trespass, the wise old man was able to confuse the mind of the magistrate in such a manner that he invariably escaped, even in the face of damning evidence of his guilt. When confronted with human beings like himself in essence, human beings that place craft on the throne of justice, no matter what social rank, power or wealth that they held, he was cold, at ease and resourceful in their presence, realising that they were inferior to himself in craft and subtlety. But here he was faced with something he did not understand and something that belonged undoubtedly to the world of superstition and mysticism, which was the only thing he feared.

Lawless folded his arms on his chest and stood opposite Macanasa.

'Tell me,' he said quietly. 'Have you people hated me, then, since I came here?'

Macanasa looked up. The expression of simplicity and innocence in Lawless's eyes again disconcerted him. It was the face of a holy monk. And the old man wondered how such a face could be possessed by a man in the devil's power, or in league with fairies. Looking at the face he remembered the human skull and he thought: 'It is mad the man is.'

'Sure we didn't hate ye now,' he said. 'But it's this way. This is a queer world and there are queer people in it. And the poor are always persecuted by the powers that be. And sure the only thing a poor man has is his bit of land that he tills with his two hands to get a bite for himself and his children. We take it hard to lose the land, Mr.–. And what do they call ye now?'

He knew the name very well, but for reasons of strategy he affected ignorance of it.

'Lawless.'

'Mr. Lawless. I'm glad to make yer acquaintance. Well, that's how it is.'

'So you are vexed because I took this land.'

'Well, that's not the way I'd put it, Mr. Lawless, because sure ye paid lashings of money for it, and an elegant gentleman like yerself wouldn't do anything unlawful. But ye see this land used to belong to a cousin of mine and she – ye might as well say it, although there was no will – she left me the land. But as there wasn't the written word that they want in the courts of law, Mr. Dolan, the shopkeeper there below, took it from me. So I went into Dublin to see the parliament men, and they all told me to see the head man of the lot, the man that has control over the giving of the land and the collecting of the rents since Lord Marley had to sell out by force. But I could get no farther than the secretary man, and he said the head man was travelling somewhere collecting information. But I think he was just hiding under the table all the time for fear I'd give him the weight of my tongue. Oh! Mr. Lawless, there are a terrible lot of ruffians among those parliament men and their secretaries. They're robbing us. And we owned all this glen one time. So we did. We were robbed of it and we're still being robbed of it by the parliament men and the shopkeepers and the...'

He had become very excited, and now he got to his feet, spat on his stick and cried in a fierce voice: 'Robbers! That's what they are.'

'I see,' said Lawless. 'I am sorry I have injured you. Forgive me.'

'Now rest in peace,' said the old man. 'It's not you. Sure how did you know? So I don't grudge it to ye. Indeed, may the good God send ye good crops and fat cattle.'

'Crops,' said Lawless. 'I don't want the land for that purpose. I'm not going to till it.'

'Ha!' said the old man eagerly. 'Is it grazing cattle yer going in for?'

'No, no,' said Lawless. 'I have no cattle, only my goats.'

'Well, then, maybe it's bees yer going to keep, or maybe it's mines yer after. They say there's gold somewhere hidden.' The old man's face became cunning and very excited.

'No,' said Lawless, with a smile. 'I am not going to use this land for anything like that. I just want it as a space about me, you see ' – he made a gesture – 'As a sort of ...

you see...' He waved his arms again, flushed, and became silent with embarrassment.

Macanasa leaned on his stick and examined him curiously. At first there was suspicion in the old man's face, and he thought: 'Could it be gold that he had heard of and he trying to hide it?' But immediately his shrewd mind saw that Lawless was hiding nothing. So he shrugged his shoulders and said: 'So ye just want room to walk about like?'

'Yes, that's it.'

'Ha!' said Macanasa, 'And if it's no harm asking ye, is it a man of learning ye are, same as Dr. Stevens that lives beyond the river in Mary Broderick's house, him that does be poking about the river looking for queer stones?'

Lawless opened his lips to speak, made a gesture, but said nothing. The old man waited for a few moments and then continued:

'Or maybe it's pictures ye make. There are two elegant gentlemen up the lake road that make darling pictures. There is a lot of money given for pictures they tell me. Fifty pounds, praise be to God, as much as that they tell me. Or maybe ye're one of them that write books. Sure there's a power of ways an elegant gentleman like yerself would pass the time. Eh?'

He had come close to Lawless while he was speaking, as if pursuing him in order to corner him and fall upon him. Lawless moved away to the window, tapped the panes restlessly with his fingers and then turned to the old man. He was very excited. He was trying to say something and yet unable to say it. The old man, as if attracted irresistibly, began to approach again. Lawless held up his hand to hold him back.

'I don't want you people to hate me,' he said gently. 'I want to be loved by you so that your love may help me fulfil my mission.' He paused, touched his forehead with his right palm, and said: 'Do you believe in God?'

Macanasa took off his hat and crossed himself after a moment's hesitation: 'Blessed be His Holy Name.'

'You do,' said Lawless intently. 'I have come here to find God. To purify my soul in solitude in order that I may understand Him. You believe without understanding,' he added in a soft whisper, gazing at Macanasa's face dreamily.

The old man began to move backwards towards the door. Lawless stopped speaking and looked ecstatically at the blank wall. He seemed unaware of the old man's presence. The old man was about to move out the door, but he changed his mind. He shut one eye and shrugged in a curious manner, as if shaking off some influence or fear. 'Ye're an innocent man,' he said, 'and ye want to be careful of the people here. They are lying thieves here and mean scoundrels. They are a sneaking, tell-tale lot and the police grow fat on them. There isn't a dog without a licence in the glen on account of the dirty daylight robbers. My own son Tom had to drown a dog in the black lake –'

'Hush,' said Lawless, suddenly recovering himself. 'This glen is a holy place, I feel it.'

'It's not the place, Mr. Lawless. It's the people that's in it. Ye want to keep an eye on them and not to let them hear ye say what ye said to me just now. Because they have no understanding, and they'll say ye're sold to the devil and they'll warn Fr. Raverty. But I'll stand by ye, Mr. Lawless.'

Lawless looked at him in pain. His hands were twitching. 'What have I said?' he whispered.

'Nothing at all, Mr. Lawless,' said the old man in a fawning voice. 'But they might make out that ye cast spells or something like that. There's a power of fairies in this glen and the people do be afraid of them.' The old man looked about him cautiously, and then coming closer, he whispered: 'This is not the time to be talking about them when the sun is up. At night they come. At night.'

'Yes,' said Lawless.

They looked at one another in silence. Then the old man changed his tone. 'I must be going now, for I have to turn the horses back. And that reminds me. I beg yer pardon, Mr. Lawless, but my horses strayed on to yer land to graze. They're wild and we can't keep them with the fences low. But maybe, seeing that ye say ye don't want the land for any purpose, ye wouldn't mind them grazing on yer share.'

'Let them graze there. Send all your cattle here to graze. It's a favour. Anything I have is yours and everybody's.'

'The land here,' said the old man, 'Bridget Macanasa's land. Ye said ye didn't...'

'Yes, yes, I don't want it. It's merely my cloister.'

'What's that?'

'You'll have it when I've done with it. It won't be long.'

'Ye mean you're going to sell it again. Indeed sure this glen is no fit place...'

The old man suddenly took his hand and kissed it reverently. 'God bless ye,' he said. 'Ye're a holy man, surely. A holy man.'

He moved hurriedly towards the door. At the doorstep he turned again, and said in a loud voice: 'A holy man.' Then he waved his stick and went out muttering prayers. But passing the goats in the yard, he crossed himself and went by stealthily. They raised their heads and watched him with their subtle eyes until he passed out the gate. He looked back from without the gate. The unicorn snorted angrily. Macanasa scowled, then crossed the little stream and hurried up the mountain at a great pace towards his horses. Now and again he paused to strike at a gorse blossom and muttered something. He was thinking furiously.

CHAPTER III

When Macanasa left the house, Lawless sat on the stool, placed his head between his hands and began to weep. For one month this was the first human being to whom he had spoken. During that time of solitude he had thought himself freed from the instinctive suspicion and fear with which human beings approach one another. And yet he had found himself, while talking to the old man, embarrassed, ashamed of announcing his purpose, suspicious of the old man's designs. He had seen in him the same tendencies towards evil that he had seen in all men hitherto, and which had made him restless and unhappy. He had seen greed, cunning and a gross pre-occupation with ephemeral ambitions. And he, therefore, knew that he himself still possessed the instincts of greed, cunning and mean vanities. So he wept to humiliate himself.

But his tears did not console him. Instead, he was assailed by a terrible uncertainty that paralysed his mind. He started, raised his head and cried in a terror-stricken voice:

'Does anything exist? Is this a mirage? Do I live?'

He listened and the subdued, seemingly distant sounds of the wilderness became uncouth to his ears. Suddenly he wanted to rise up and fly to the city, where he might riot his senses among accustomed sounds, gay pleasures and companionship. But he did not rise, for his mind had travelled into the city before his muscles had obeyed his will to make him move. And there it found memories still more revolting than its present fear of the wilderness.

'That is infinitely worse,' he murmured. 'Can I have forgotten all the miseries of that debased existence so soon that I want to return to it? Am I so weak, I who consider myself capable of reaching that goal that no man yet has reached? Neither Christ, nor Buddha, nor all the holy seers and prophets.'

His despair gave way to an exaltation that was of equal magnitude; his eyes, glistening with tears, became brilliant with joy. His heart beat wildly and he experienced the eager passion with which a lover awaits the coming of a dearly beloved mistress. He found himself listening for something.

For what? He did not know. He could not describe what he expected. But it seemed that it rested at a distance, crystallised into a form, although it was a formless thing, by the intensity of his longing. It was afar off, in the distant sky, moving in the void of the universe, surrounded with a mist and he dared not look towards it. He must sit waiting its coming. He struggled fiercely to attract it by concentrating all the forces of his being on its contemplation. It did not come nearer. Instead it drifted away, becoming smaller and smaller until it became a point. And as it decreased, his happiness grew less and less, until he suffered pain instead of joy. Then all feeling left him and he contemplated the point in peace.

The universe had resolved itself into a single point. Just as the point had begun to expand, he grew tired watching it. In spite of his efforts, ideas floated into his mind. Sounds became audible. He slowly awoke from his ecstasy and became fully aware of the world about him. He leaned his head sideways and rested it on his right hand. He sighed, disheartened. As yet nothing had been made manifest.

After a while he realised that no previous ecstasy had been so powerful or sudden as this one. At no other time had the material world and the consciousness of material things been so completely submerged in the contempation of universal unity. This realisation cheered him. Like a man who has gained a minor victory and feels himself approaching the goal of his ambitions, his mind looked back with joy over the road he had travelled.

Thirty years ago he had been born on his father's estate in the west of Ireland. While still very young, he became aware of the extreme poverty of the peasants who paid rent to his father. He saw the hovels in which they lived, their starved bodies, the brooding look of malice in their eyes. And it made him very unhappy. Then he began to realise that these people looked upon him and his family as their enemies. He felt shame as well as unhappiness, because he thought his father was the cause of the people's suffering. That was why his father lived apart from the people and despised them; while they, in turn, feared and hated him. As he grew into a lad, he tried to associate with the young peasants, but he always found an invisible barrier between him and them. This barrier grew greater as he grew older, into the image and likeness of their master. Then he went to university.

There he joined a group of students who wished to organise a revolution in order to free the people. For this he was arrested by the police, expelled from the university and tried in a public court of law. His father influenced the authorities to let him go free. The young man returned home in disgrace; and shortly afterwards his father died, probably of a broken heart, because of the insult offered to his family pride by his son's treason against his caste.

As there were no other sons in the family, Lawless inherited the estate. His mother and his two sisters had been separately provided for in the will. The estate, houses, carriages, horses and other values came into Henry's possession. Immediately he decided to distribute it all among the peasants.

His relatives raised an outcry, but nothing could hinder the young man's purpose. He handed over the land to an elected committee of the people, with a request that particular attention should be paid to the claims of the very poor who were without any land hitherto. But instead of distributing the land equitably among one another, the peasants quarrelled violently. Each man was so greedy that he desired it all for himself. Those who had land already resisted with great violence and indignation the claims of their landless brethren, while the very poor sold their interest in the land to the local shopkeeping usurer and spent the proceeds in drunkenness and dissipation. Unheard of crimes were committed in the neighbourhood, and these poor people, who hitherto seemed deserving of a just man's pity, now showed traits of greed, lechery and malice that horrified all. And, curiously enough, those who committed the most gross acts themselves were most violent in denouncing the greed and turpitude of their neighbours. Until finally the poor people found themselves in a worse position than their previous one, for they were now slaves to many masters instead of being slaves to one master. Lawyers had fattened on their quarrels. Shopkeepers and moneylenders had become enriched, and the priests owned motor cars, having received large presents both as thanks and offerings from those who had enriched themselves and as peace offerings from those who had committed crimes.

Lawless was so overwhelmed by this disaster that he lost all belief in the goodness of humanity. All his love of justice and righteousness withered. Instead of giving away his houses, his horses and his remaining property, he sold them all by public auction. Then he cursed bitterly and left the district, determined that nothing was worth while and that the only sane purpose in life was self-amusement. He travelled about from country to country, amusing himself with women, art, gambling and dissipation of every kind that man has hitherto invented. Then having spent all his money and being still unhappy he returned to Ireland to put an end to his life.

Fortunately, a war was in progress when he returned; and it seemed an impossibility for the young man to kill himself voluntarily while a war was in progress. In war almost every conviction held previous to the outbreak of hostilities suffers a reaction. And amidst the feverish energy that is squandered on all sides, the very depths of human emotions are stirred violently, to give birth to fantastic religions, enthusiasms and lusts. Lawless had become completely detached from the people and from his revolutionary enthusiasm by the disillusionment resulting from the division of his property. His idealism had been smothered by his dissipation. Now, in this war of liberation carried on by the people against the Government, he merely saw an attempt by the remainder of the peasantry to acquire land and wealth, and he felt that the attempt if successful would bring more suffering, greed and corruption. So, instead of killing himself, he went about among the people exhorting them to cease fighting.

Very soon the soldiers of the Republican Army arrested him as a spy, claiming that nobody but a spy could be guilty of preaching the doctrines of Christ during a war. He was brought as a prisoner to a cave in a mountainous district, under the control of some men who treated him kindly until they could get official permission to put him to death. There, however, he was captured by a platoon of English soldiers, who imprisoned both him and his guards in a Government internment camp, for his strange doctrines of the futility of strife appeared as pernicious to the Government troops as they had appeared to the revolutionaries. He remained interned until the end of the war, when he was released with the others.

During his internment his philosophy of peace and his glorification of poverty found favour among his fellow prisoners; for being poor and in danger of execution, they were ready to believe that all men should be poor and free from the danger of a violent death. Then after the truce and the release of the prisoners, he was brought by these men as a comrade to a Republican training camp in the mountains. Here his gentle nature, his idealism and his refined manners endeared him to the soldiers and he began to feel happy. Excited by the good moral effect his teachings appeared to have on the soldiers, he also began to believe that he was a teacher divinely appointed to lead the people.

But soon the war broke out afresh between those who favoured peace with England and those who favoured a continuation of the war with that country. The supporters of the peace claimed that it would bring material prosperity. They were accused by their Republican opponents of materialism, greed and treachery. The Republicans, on the other hand, were called dreamers and blood-thirsty anarchists, who wanted to turn the country into a desert. Again Lawless found himself in a difficulty. He favoured the asceticism advocated by the Republicans. But he also favoured the peace advocated by their opponents. So that he was again denounced as a traitor by the Republicans who preached asceticism and war; while he was imprisoned as a dangerous character by the new Government, who advocated peace and enrichment as the goal of life.

This time he made no friends in jail. For twelve months he thought in the solitude of his cell. But even though he had suffered greater disappointment by preaching universal benevolence than he had suffered by giving away his property, he did not despair as a result of his fresh disillusionment. On the contrary, his soul was cast down into those depths where fresh courage is gathered for a greater flight. In solitude and contemplation he disburdened his mind of all beliefs, to prepare it for the creation of fresh beliefs and discoveries. For the first time he became inspired with a free and questioning consciousness of the universe. Hitherto he had followed the dogmas of men who had gone before him. Now he realised that man must doubt everything before knowing anything. And he became convinced that man had never known God and that his efforts towards the attainment of happiness and beauty had failed hitherto through ignorance of their source. So he set himself the task of finding God.

Finally he was released from jail, some time after the conclusion of hostilities, on the solicitation of his elder sister. The prison governor, on releasing him, handed him a letter from his sister. It contained a banker's cheque for four hundred pounds and a note which abused him roundly, accusing him of having ruined his family and sent both his father and his mother to an early grave. 'I am sending you this money,' she concluded, 'in order that you may go to the farthest corner of the earth, if you have a spark of honour left.'

Lawless experienced neither sorrow nor joy on reading the letter; for even though he loved his family and especially his mother, his mother's death did not seem to him a disaster, since he felt she must be obviously happier in the Heaven in which she fervently believed than on this earth, which had brought her a great deal of sorrow. The money he accepted with gratitude, because it enabled him to carry out his purpose.

He rented a furnished cottage not very far from Dublin and began to prepare himself for a life of sanctity. But he did not stay long in this first place, as it was situated in a thickly populated district where the people made fun of his eccentricities and molested him in many ways. The police also insisted on worrying him, being under the impression that he was still a dangerous revolutionary. He purchased two goats from a neighbour who was ill-treating the animals. The goats rapidly became very fond of him, but the people raised an outcry and said he was possessed of the devil. The proprietor of the cottage then dismissed him from his tenancy at short notice, suggesting that the house in the Fairy Glen, which had just been advertised, would suit him much better. In that manner, Lawless at last became the proprietor of the red-roofed house in the Fairy Glen.

Although he had formerly considered himself the most hapless and persecuted of all mankind, he now saw in the various incidents of his career a necessary preparation for the great task before him. His jaws set and his body became rigid. He shuddered violently and jumped to his feet. He threw his arms over his head and uttered a low cry of joy. His face grew radiant. He threw back his head and listened eagerly to the murmur of bees, to the warbling of birds, to the distant calls of animals, to the rumbling of a far-off cart on the mountain road. And he became exalted with the joy of life and the consciousness that he was free, free to love, to live in solitude. Clasping his hands on his bosom he murmured:

'I am free. I am free. Eternal beauty, I approach thee. I come, trembling with love.'

Then he went out of the house eagerly into the yard. He called his goats. He heard them bleat in answer, but for a moment he could not see them, for they had mounted the fence, one on either side of the gate, and the naughty beasts were devouring the hawthorn blossoms. As if shaken by a wind, the blossoms fell from the branches in a white shower and the brown backs of the goats were strewn with them. Then the goats thrust out their heads and looked at him. He became very angry and rushed forward to strike them; but seeing him come thus angrily, the unicorn jumped down from the fence and came sidling towards him, bleating timorously, with lowered head. Then he saw the bare stump of the horn that had been knocked off by the boor who formerly possessed her, and his anger left him. He stroked her head and said: 'Why must you eat those white blossoms that are the image of God? Is it because man has injured you?'

The goat raised her head and looked into his eyes. Then she bleated and raising her tail and her front legs, she pretended to buffet him with her arched head. The bald goat also jumped from the fence, snorted and bounded away to the right towards the river. The unicorn pursued her with loud cries.

He followed them at a run and jumped the fence to the rear of the house. He raced down the slope towards the river, along the sunny grass, gambolling with the merry animals. The goats ran so fast that milk squirted from their teats, and it was truly a strange sight, as if some occult force had suddenly taken possession of both man and animals.

A small group of peasants witnessed the scene from a hillock to the left, beside Deegan's field of young oats that was still green and grass-like. There were four men there and two women, gathered about old Macanasa, who was gesticulating with his short stick and talking earnestly. Deegan was there with his stout wife, and the other peasant who lived to the left of the red-roofed house was also there with his wife. A very old man leaning on two sticks, Deegan's father, stood in the background; while Macanasa's eldest son, lean like a rye stalk, knelt on one knee with a shepherd's crooked stick in his hand. When they saw Lawless and the goats running they all stood up and closed in on one another, and shielding their eyes against the sun, they gazed after him with frightened faces. And old Macanasa said in a whisper:

'Eh? Was it the truth I told ye now? Eh?'

Lawless did not see them; but running down towards the little bridge he suddenly met another man, who came running towards him along the hither bank of the river from the left, among tall ferns. This was a short man, wearing a fisherman's wading kit and carrying in his hand a landing net. He had a round, gentle face which bore a curious smile as he approached. As soon as he saw Lawless, he paused, panted and then called out in an excited voice, as he wiped his brow with his sleeve:

'Excuse me, but did you by any chance see a black butterfly pass you just now?'

CHAPTER IV

Passion is innocent of shame. Lovers embrace on the highways. Religious fanatics lacerate their nakedness in the grottoes of their saints. Topers confess tearfully in the drinking shops what they have pawned for liquor. So, the most intense of all passions, the lust of knowledge, makes a timorous man as innocently daring as a year-old babe that seizes all things in its chubby fists to test their flavour on the dribbling palate.

Dr. Edward Stevens, whom Lawless met on the river bank chasing a black butterfly, was a man of withdrawn temperament, who blushed at a woman's smile or at a word of praise from a fellow man. A man of genius, he shirked the public pursuit of his profession lest it might bring him into vulgar contact with society. Owing to his poverty he had been a lecturer for some years at a university, until, by a lucky chance, he invented a patent for extracting sardines from a box in such a manner that the fishes came forth intact. This trivial discovery brought him a yearly income sufficient to support his life without the necessity of working for a salary. He therefore retired to the glen in order to enjoy in peace his solitary passion.

This passion was an intense curiosity: so intense that it had no apparent purpose. Peasant women in lonely villages are very often driven through boredom to listening at their neighbours' doors; and these women, though in the beginning they are inclined to traffic in scandalous gossip, become in time very secretive about their clandestine discoveries. The act of satisfying their curiosity by listening becomes so delicious that the act of imparting the knowledge gained to their neighbours, though usually the most pleasant part of the transaction, loses its interest entirely. In the same manner, Dr. Stevens ravenously collected in the glen all manner of information, but he made no apparent use of it. He wrote it down in large notebooks and there it remained. Birds, beasts, men, stones, herbs, flowers, currents of air, clouds, the elements, abstract theories of existence, of religion and of philosophy all interested him equally. He was interested in art, literature, politics, sociology, history and every new direction of human thought. But his mind seemed to have no faculty for measuring the relative values of any two ideas, discoveries or facts; so that a brown mole on a peasant's left ear was as important and interesting to him as the discovery of radium, the Russian Revolution or the crucifixion of Jesus Christ.

His habits of thought had freed him from all convictions, beliefs and inhibitions; for as all things, even the most fantastic thoughts, became real and substantial objects in his imagination, the mental attitude of reverence, which is the necessary quality of belief, was impossible for him. A child, looking at a king, sees only the king's body and is interested only if there is a large wart or some other excrescence on the king's countenance; or if, like the good king Dagobert, his majesty has his trousers on back to front. Stevens, although his intellect was powerful and mature, resembled a child in this respect, seeing everything in its exact proportions.

He owed his excellent health to his curiosity; for irregularities of his organs aroused such interest in him that he immediately took steps to set them in order, simply to discover what had gone wrong and what was the correct remedy.

When the two men met on the river bank they stared at one another with great interest. Although they were both shy of their fellow men, each saw in the other's countenance his own shyness. The gentle, rather childish face of the scientist attracted Lawless, who loved gentleness in others because he fostered it in himself as the supreme virtue. Stevens saw in the ascetic, brooding face of Lawless a fresh phenomenon: and he immediately forgot the black butterfly in order to pursue this fresh object. As a result of this mutual interest, neither spoke for some time: and yet neither felt embarrassment.

At last Stevens abruptly took a cigarette case from his pocket and offered Lawless a cigarette. It was only then that Lawless remembered the question he had been asked. Waving aside the proffered cigarette, he said: 'No, I haven't seen a butterfly. But why do you ask?'

'Do you smoke?'

Lawless shook his head.

Stevens put a cigarette between his lips. 'It's of no consequence. It's gone by now. A very interesting specimen. You see, I put this net over it and observe, just like this –' He put the landing net, mouth downwards, over a little gorse bush. 'Just so. Excellent idea. You observe them both resting and on the wing.'

Lawless furrowed his forehead and frowned. 'Very cruel,' he said.

Stevens's face altered. He had curious heavy dark eyebrows that joined over his short nose, giving his face, when intent, the appearance of a satyr. 'Why do you think it's cruel?'

'Surely the butterfly is terrified when he tries to fly away and finds the net over him?'

'Children are terrified by thunder,' said Stevens. 'Yet thunder is not cruel.'

'But surely you realise the difference between a conscious act and the blind act of nature?'

'I don't know that nature is blind,' said Stevens.

Lawless looked at him in surprise. Their eyes met. Lawless shuddered before the intent gaze of the scientist.

'You mean to say,' he said, 'that – you believe thunder is the conscious act of some –'

'No, quite wrong,' said Stevens. 'I don't say I believe. I simply don't know that thunder is not the conscious act of some –'

'Some what?' said Lawless eagerly. Again they looked one another in the eyes.

'Are you the new tenant of that red-roofed house over there?' asked Stevens.

'Yes.'

'I intended calling on you.'

'I'm sorry,' said Lawless abruptly, 'I'm not receiving visitors.'

'Oh, pardon me.' Stevens moved away.

'Stay... One moment. Forgive me. I have a reason. I must explain to you that I –'

Stevens paused, looked at Lawless and smiled.

'Do you mind,' said Lawless, 'Who are you?'

'My name is Stevens. I live in that cottage.' He pointed to a little house across the river to the right.

'Are you, too, a recluse?' asked Lawless in a low voice.

'No, not exactly, I just live here in order to – why simply because I – well, as a matter of fact I am interested in a certain theory and I have chosen this glen as a particularly suitable place to make observations.'

Lawless's face brightened. 'That's very interesting,' he said shyly. 'I wonder if you, too, are - But no! Why should you persecute the – Forgive me. I hope I have not hurt your feelings in any way. Let me explain. My name is Lawless.' He paused and flushed. Just at that moment the goats came up chewing some leaves. They snorted at the doctor. Lawless smiled and seemed to gather courage from their presence. 'Why should I not tell you?' he said seriously and in a low voice. 'I have come into this glen in order to find God.'

Stevens dropped his cigarette on to the ground in amazement. Then he stooped, as if to pick it up, but really that Lawless might not notice his embarrassment. Instead, he plucked a blade of grass and put it between his lips.

'I see,' said Stevens. 'In other words, you are making religious experiments.'

Lawless started from his ecstatic reverie. 'Experiments!' he said in surprise. 'What do you mean?'

Stevens coughed out the blade of grass he had begun to chew. Now they both became embarrassed. Each instinctively realised that the other was an enemy, in that unexplainable way in which two human beings, by means of a word, or a glance, or a subconscious smell, realise that there is a spiritual antagonism between them. And then each, through courtesy, tried to hide this knowledge from the other, even though each knew that the other knew.

'I cannot escape him,' thought Lawless.

'He's an interesting character,' thought Stevens.

'Are these your goats?' said Stevens aloud, in a polite, casual tone.

'Yes.'

'Beautiful creatures. Curious eyes goats have. What would a woman not give for such subtlety of expression?' With that Stevens smiled, bowed slightly, murmured something and walked away.

Lawless moved towards the bridge, followed by his goats. When Stevens had gone a short distance, he paused, plucked another blade of grass to chew and turned around to observe the retreating figure of Lawless. Lawless crossed the bridge and then moved slowly to the left with downcast head, with his arms close by his sides and the palms of his hands extended horizontally as if he were cautioning something to be still.

While Stevens watched, a small group of peasants approached him, led by old Patrick Macanasa. They were also watching the retreating figure of Lawless. Macanasa saw Stevens and saluted him. Stevens nodded and said: 'I have some tobacco for you. Come up to the house later.'

'Thanks your honour,' said Macanasa.

Although Stevens had spoken in a low voice, the old man, usually deaf, heard him at a distance.

Standing beside Macanasa, there was a tall slim woman with very dark straight hair that hung, bedraggled, around her passionate long face. She was Mrs. Dillon, the wife of a ragged peasant who stood in the background, with a hook of some sort on his shoulder. The young woman was eagerly polite, watching the retreating figure of Lawless, and as she watched, her delicate nostrils quivered, her red lips were opened, and there was a curious brilliant light in her large eyes.

'He's a decent man, Dr. Stevens,' said Macanasa, pointing after Lawless.

'Do you know him?' said Stevens, casually, looking at the young woman, sideways.

The young woman looked secretly at the doctor, with a cunning expression in her eyes. Then she bit her lower lip, winked her right eye very quickly and turned to her husband: 'Come on, Barney,' she said. 'It's time to be going.'

The others gathered around Macanasa, who was talking in a low voice to Dr. Stevens.

'It's the war,' said Macanasa, 'is the cause of it. They do be queer in the head.'

'God! He's stripping off his clothes,' said Deegan. 'Is it going to drown himself he is?'

They all looked excitedly.

Down on the green smooth meadow there was a low mound below the bridge at the far bank of the river. Then the river twisted sharply to the right, down a little gorge, between a rock and a short, stout tree, whose branches dipped their trailing leafy twigs into the river foam. Then it widened into a deep brown pool of still water, with the current moving in little eddies down the centre. Along the left bank of the long pool there were over-arching trees. And the right bank was bare. The pool had a bed of yellow sand, that glistened with the silvery scales of fish. Little herds of minnows scurried about its shallows, while trout stood at intervals, steering themselves with their swift tails; or darted in and out among the trees.

On the little mound, Lawless took off his clothes and then descended naked into the pool. He waded out into the centre where the water reached his armpits. Then he dived to the bottom, arose again and crossing his arms on his chest, he stood still. The goats came to the upright brow of the bank and watched him. A small herd of cattle, grazing on the meadow, languid with the noonday heat, began to approach, moving slowly, halting, smelling, moving, blowing rheumy air from their enormous wet nostrils and staring with their foolish eyes. Cunning little birds, perched in the still branches of the trees, made questioning sounds and craned their necks to see the white naked skin of the man above the water and his yellow skin under water. A wild duck flopped on to a rock afar down the river, jerked its neck up and down fiercely, and seeing the man with a single circular eye in its turned head, screamed wildly and barged in flight through dry brambles high into the empty air.

Still, still and happy as a child dreaming in its mother's fondling arms, was the air, the earth, the running water of the river.

He stood still, and suddenly it was made manifest to him that there was great virtue in his body. Suddenly his body enshrouded his soul, and he was aware that it was beautiful. He became aware that it was holy. He became aware, calmly, of many things. Without looking or seeing with his eyes, he saw the group of people watching him. He also saw the beasts and birds watching him. And presently down in the water, he saw a beautiful speckled trout, with rainbow tints on its smooth pelt, emerge from a tree sideways and pause, watching him.

'Why do they all watch me?' Lawless thought of Dr. Stevens, whose unpleasant influence he had been trying to dispel as he walked down the river bank. He had been afraid the doctor was laughing at him. Now he saw the doctor differently. Strange! All men seemed reduced to puny size, looking up at him. He felt himself grow to a wonderful size.

He looked down at his feet immersed in the water. They had grown many times their size. And stranger still, their colour had changed. They were almost the colour of the yellow sand, but of a translucent hue. He closed his eyes and moving his hands, he felt the tender heat of his body, the smooth skin and the soft throbbing motion of his chest. And a delicious rapture overspread his being. Then he cast his thoughts into the heavens, where he had hitherto sought for God. Without looking, he could sense a pleasant vastness there, where hitherto there had been an unpleasant emptiness which it was imperative to fill and organise in proper manner. Now, quite near, he felt an immeasurable, perhaps infinite, power.

It was so wonderful that he ceased thinking. He even lost all sensibility. River flies now settled on his body, irritating his skin by their crawling legs, and yet he did not feel them. Prostrate mentally by the discovery that the great infinite thing was not above in the void, unseen and unknown, but near himself, he felt nothing.

Now he opened his eyes and looked at the water. How calm and happy he had become! So calm and happy that his face shone. There was a flush on either cheek as on the cheeks of a bride approaching the bridal bed.

The water was pleasantly warm. The over-arching trees deflected the direct downpour of the hot sun-rays. It was silent, as in an empty, locked room. The goats, tired of watching, began to move about. He did not notice them, even though they bleated querulously. The cattle came nearer, moving step by step, their muscles creaking, swinging their tails and licking their sides with their coarse tongues. A little bird, through curiosity, fluttered out and attempted to alight on his head; but took fright and passed rapidly, in undulating stretches of flight, away up the mountain side.

All the people had gone to their homes for their noon-day meal. Afar off, Dr. Stevens emerged from the door of his cottage. He put a field glass to his eyes and remained still for a long time, watching the spot where Lawless was standing in the stream. He could only see Lawless's head. The head was motionless. The doctor lowered the instrument, rubbed his chin and passed into the cottage. A large woman, the wife of Deegan the peasant, was coming up the glen along the left bank of the river towards her home, after visiting a sick relative. She saw Lawless standing still with his hands stretched out in front of him as if giving a blessing. She crept up secretly behind the bushes and trees that lined the river bank, until she came quite close, standing in a green barley field. Her great maternal face, red and large-eyed, became full of wonder. Big with child, her hands clasped with difficulty over her broad figure. Her eyes glowed as she watched and she strained forward towards him. Then suddenly she turned, raised her skirts and walked heavily through the barley, trampling the young shoots in her excitement. Afar off, her little sons called her, clamouring for food.

Old Macanasa now appeared, leaning over the fence of his yard, chewing bread and staring downwards anxiously at the little mound on which the clothes were strewn.

Suddenly the cattle rushed forward in a body and chased the goats. The goats fled. The cattle then stared at

Lawless. First one beast and then another came to the river bank, smelling. Still Lawless was not aware of their presence. They began to smell his clothes. Then a speckled cow picked up his belt and began to chew it. The other cattle watched and then they all reached for it. Two beasts seized it in their jaws and hauled at it. Soon there was a wild struggle. The horns of the contending beasts rattled and their hoofs tore up the earth; until, just as suddenly, they all took fright and raced away to a distance. The speckled cow still held the belt, half swallowed, with its end, froth-covered, trailing.

Still Lawless did not move. He was completely wrapt in an ecstasy. He was, in fact, now afraid to move, because the newly-discovered holiness of his body inspired such awe in him that he felt it would be sacriligeous to move his limbs.

The cow began to moan, tossing her head, trying to reject the belt, which at first she had tried to swallow.

Old Macanasa hurried down the mountain-side to the cow, uttering loud cries. The cow was coughing with her head to the ground. He caught the end of the belt and pulled it forth. Then he beat the cow's side with his stick and drove her up the meadow. Then he came to the river bank, with the belt, muttering. When he saw Lawless standing still in the water, he halted.

'Mr. Lawless.'

Lawless did not move. The old man came slowly to the little mound where the clothes were strewn. He looked down, leaning his hand on his knee.

'Mr. Lawless,' he said again, speaking in a whisper.

Lawless did not move, but his right shoulder trembled slightly.

'I declare to God,' said the old man in surprise, 'it's asleep he is.'

'Have ye got a cramp?' he cried in a loud voice.

Lawless turned his head slowly, and when the old man saw his strange exalted countenance, he became afraid.

Lawless looked at him calmly, s[illegible]
up the belt.

'The cows were eating it,' he said. [illegible]
leave yer clothes in the field.'

'Fear nothing,' said Lawless in a strange voi[illegible]

The old man dropped the belt and wiped his fin[illegible]
the grass.

'River water is dangerous,' he said. 'Ye shouldn't stay
so long in it. Ye've been there nearly three hours. Ye'll
catch yer death.'

Lawless started, and suddenly he began to tremble
with cold. His lips became pale and his teeth began to
chatter slightly. 'Death,' he said, 'there is no such thing.'

Then he waded out. The old man, lest he might see the
other's nakedness, turned his head and hurried away.

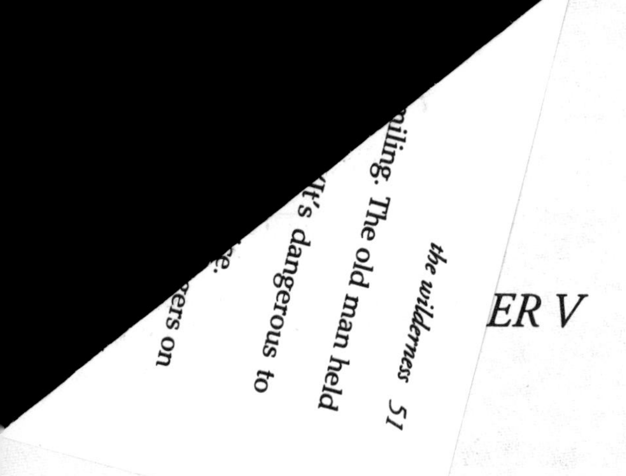

ER V

The sun set slowly. The mountain peaks became red. A yellow glow suffused the surface of the lowland earth. The departing rays of light seemed to flit among the tree branches, scintillating with many unexpected colours. All sounds became subdued, and there was a throbbing expectancy in the air; as when a master hand plucks with a bow the first tender notes of a great score from a delicate instrument. And then came music more gently sweet than any of man's creation. It was the lowing of homing cows, always distant. Amorous pigeons cooed their silly notes hidden in tree branches. Little sheep, moving like rolling white dots, bleated for their lambs. And high over all the many sounds, the blackbirds, lords of the sunset, made the valley ring with their melodies.

Peasants who had idled all the summer day were now busy; for even in mid-summer, the peasant's holiday time, the hour of home-coming is the occasion of great activity and joyous shouting.

Three generations were labouring around Deegan's cottage. The little house lay at the end of a rough track that descended from the mountain road between steep banks that were lined with bracken. From a distance it seemed entirely surrounded with rocky land and a wild growth of bracken. Scattered at intervals around the house were little fields reclaimed by industrious ancestors from the wilderness. There was a deep yard, like a pit, paved with cobblestones. A high wall of granite boulders surrounded the yard, like the wall of a prehistoric fort. There were several ungainly outhouses. Poultry, pigs, cattle, horses and goats roamed about. In the yard, the old grandfather chopped wood slowly with a small axe: his slow hands handling the blocks clumsily; a little boy of fourteen months stumbled about on his stomach near the old man, catching at twigs, struggling to his feet unsteadily and then falling foolishly on his buttocks. Two bigger boys rushed about shouting loudly, with rods, herding cows into their shed to be milked. The grandmother, wearing a man's cap, held a dish over her head, from which she scattered food to a flock of hens that scurried about her feet, in a thick mass of fluttering wings, jabbing beaks and scratching legs. Mrs. Deegan, moving corpulently, opened the door of the pig shed, and emptied the pot of food into the trough. There was a wild scramble of pigs and then fierce screeches, as the surly brutes tore at one another's ears in their eagerness to get at the food.

It was a joyous scene. Yet each living thing was hurrying angrily. The beasts and fowls buffeted one another and the human beings bore the dour look of intensity that accompanies fear, greed and lechery. But the same look accompanies, at times, the acts of greatest heroism, virtue and creative ecstasy. Here there was the primitive simplicity and beauty of labour, performed with fierce enthusiasm by individuals that worked for no personal reward but through the primeval instinct of the preservation of the family. The lashing of the cows by the sturdy boys, the savage biting and screeching of the pigs, the decrepit grandparents tottering with old age, still moving to their infant tasks, the hard face of the child-carrying mother, were all unified into a single glorious act, when seen as the material and root of human greatness; the struggle for bread and conquest.

The turmoil subsided as the fowls and beasts were fed and housed. Then Mrs. Deegan said in an angry voice:

'Where's your father?'

Immediately the two little boys ran in their bare feet to a green mound above the yard. They began to cry aloud: 'Da-a-addy! '

'Here I am,' came Deegan's voice, and presently he appeared, walking rapidly, chewing a long straw. He threw his coat on the fence of the yard and washed his rough hands in a little tub. Then he went into the byre to milk the cows. Soon the slow, purling sound of falling milk was heard, and one of the little boys standing near the milker, began to croon a milking song in imitation of his mother. The father, milking, did not croon but occasionally uttered a loud brutal warning to the cow, striking her on the side with his clenched fist. The other little boy crept close and watched the movements of the milking hand intently and begged his father to let him milk. To him the father spoke gently. But withal, his tanned, lean face looked worried and he vented his displeasure on the cow.

Their tasks finished, all went indoors, and immediately there was perfect silence around the farmhouse. Now there was only the swishing sound of woodcocks' wings flying high overhead and the distant croaking of marsh birds. Night was falling.

The old grandmother brought the infant to the fire and stripped him naked. He stretched his young limbs and, innocent of shame, he rubbed his fat stomach joyfully with his chubby hands, uttering gurgling cries. Though only fourteen months, his limbs were perfectly moulded and his long straight thighs showed promise of giant stature. His big, blue eyes were soft, merry and foolish, showing no prospect of an intelligent, ruminative mind. But already there were signs of a powerful jaw and savage strength in the broad chest and neck. Standing before the fire naked, the infant boy made them all pause to look at him. Coming in one by one, hurriedly, angrily, hungrily, they all looked, smiled and became glad; as if his young strength and his Gargantuan gestures threw a mantle of protection over their future.

'He will inherit the glen!'

The grandmother began to wash the child in a basin that was much too small for him. He stamped on the water and yelled with delight when the water splashed about the floor.

Supper was already laid on a deal table in the centre of the floor. The grandfather took his plate of potatoes and a mug of milk to his corner seat on the hearthstones. Opening his penknife he cleaned the long blade in his muffler and began to peel the potatoes slowly with it.

'Say Grace before your food,' muttered the old grandmother querulously.

The old man raised his head and looked about him anxiously. The two little boys laughed loudly, clapped their hands and cried:

'Bless yourself, grand-daddy.'

The old man smiled and struck his knee and said:

'Well! Well! I'm getting foolish sure enough. Good Virgin and your Holy Son, may the –'

Then he smiled again and forgetting the prayer which he had begun, he continued to eat without blessing himself. The two little boys were delighted at this and they continued to clap their hands and cry:

'Bless yourself, grand-daddy.'

But the old man took no heed.

'Sit down to yer supper,' cried the mother irritably.

The two little boys jumped up, rushed to the table and began to eat their food. Their father also sat down pompously and ate. The mother still hurried about setting things in order, though it was impossible to understand the purpose of her movements, owing to the immense clutter of things in the dark, dirty room. In the dim twilight the large room looked like a crowded barn, with rubbish strewn on its earthen floor, its walls crowded with pasteboard calendars, mottoes received from shopkeepers, cooking utensils, farming tools and photographs. There were benches, barrels, bags of meal, a smoked ham, a sack of flour, a heap of firewood, and a large settle bed, on top of which a bitch and two pups were sleeping. But in every corner of the room she found something to do, and although her efforts made no evident change in the appearance of the place, she worked anxiously and with purpose. At last she finished, sighed, and sat down to eat. Nobody spoke until the meal was finished. The grandmother dressed the infant, put it in a cradle and gave it its food. Then she, like the old man, took her food to the hearthstone and ate it.

The two little boys were the first to finish their supper. They brought stools to the hearth, got their satchels and began to read aloud from their school books, calling on their elders for appreciation.

'There now,' said the grandmother, 'isn't that great learning?'

Grandfather finished his supper, threw the potato skins on the floor for the bitch and then washed his plate in a basin. Then he came to the settle and beat the bitch off it. The bitch jumped down with a yelp and surprised that supper had already been served, she dashed around anxiously, trying to eat all the scraps at once. The old man placed the cubs gently on the floor, made his bed on the settle and went to bed in his clothes. Then he took off his boots after lying down and lit his pipe.

'There he is again,' said the old woman, 'gone to bed without his prayers.'

'Say your prayers, grand-daddy,' said the little boys.

The old man began to laugh foolishly and took his pipe out of his mouth.

'Let him alone now,' shouted the father.

Afraid of the father's fierce voice, the two little boys became silent again.

The mother rose and lit a paraffin lamp. That was a signal for the two little boys to mount the ladder to their bed in the loft. The old grandmother brought the cradle into a little room behind the fireplace. The husband and wife were alone. The wife cleared the table. The husband sat on a stool in front of the fire and lit his clay pipe. Night had not yet fallen completely, and an occasional distant bird piped a drowsy note. But it was very still, as at midnight.

Mrs. Deegan, having finished her work, sat in the hearth corner, clasped her hands about her knees and looked into the fire. The old man began to snore. The bitch brought her cubs to a basket in which there was straw and began to give them suck. Deegan cleared his throat and spoke.

'I was talking to Mr. Lawless,' he said.

Mrs. Deegan looked up eagerly. Then she took a halfknit sock from a hole in the chimney wall, scratched her hair with one of the needles, and began to knit.

'Aye,' she said.

'They say he's queer in the head,' continued her husband, staring with wide open mouth at the fire.

His lean, dark face was intent with fear. His high cheekbones, hollow cheeks and sharp jaws gave him a wild mountainy look. His wife looked at him shrewdly.

Beside him, she looked extremely intelligent and capable. Her square face, not without voluptuous beauty, was very masculine.

'What did he say?' she whispered casually.

Deegan got excited. He began to make gestures. 'He stopped me, an' I crossing the ford with the red horse,' he said. 'He says to put our cattle on his land.'

His wife stopped knitting and bit the end of the needle. Aye'.

'He said,' continued Deegan raising his voice excitedly, 'that he has good news for the glen an' that –'

'Hush. Don't talk so loud.'

'And that,' continued Deegan in a low whisper, 'there's going to be no more death.'

'God between us an' harm.'

The old man had stopped snoring and moved, awakened by his son's loud voice.

'That's what he said,' whispered Deegan. 'There's nobody going to die no more.'

'What's that I hear ye saying?' mumbled the old man, trying to sit up.

'Nothing, dad,' said Deegan. 'Go to sleep.'

'I thought I heard ye say,' mumbled the old man, 'that there was to be.... that nobody was goin' to.... that......' He sank back again and closed his eyes.

'Macanasa's horses and sheep are on his land,' said Mrs. Deegan. 'I suppose he knows it.'

'He says to have everybody to put their cattle,' said Deegan with great emphasis. 'He says that everybody is the same as everybody else.'

'That's queer talk,' said the woman.

'What?' said Deegan.

They looked at one another.

'Would it be right?' said Deegan fearfully. 'God between us and harm, maybe there's a curse on the land.'

'Don't be a fool,' said the woman coldly, 'ye have children to rear.'

'Woman, ye have no conscience. Same way ye wanted to buy that land before and no good came of it.'

'Because you were too cowardly to face the Macanasas,' retorted his wife. 'Tomorrow I'll put the horses on the land meself.'

'Listen – didn't ye tell me ye saw him standing in the river?'

'An' why shouldn't he stand in the river?'

'Paddy Macanasa makes out he's sold to the devil.'

'Aye, but his grass isn't, for Macanasa's horses are thriving on it.'

Suddenly the bitch began to bark.

'Lie down,' cried Deegan angrily.

The old man awoke again and said querulously:

'What's that?'

Steps approached the house and they heard a hard, dry cough.

'It's old Macanasa,' said Deegan.

'Are yez in bed?' came the voice of Macanasa at the window.

'No,' said Deegan. 'Come in Paddy.'

'Hasn't he the neck to set his dirty feet in my house,' grumbled Mrs. Deegan.

Macanasa lifted the latch, opened the door slightly and thrust in his grizzly head. He peered around.

'God save all here,' he said.

'And you, too,' said Deegan, without rising. Macanasa paused and then entered, stepping cautiously, from habit, as if he entered to steal. He closed the door behind him and came to the fire.

'I just looked in,' he said, 'to get a light for my pipe.'

'Ye're welcome,' said Deegan.

Macanasa looked from one to the other. Then, instead of taking out his pipe, he bent down close to Deegan's face and said: 'Was it you I saw talking to Mr. Lawless by the ford?'

'And what of it?' said Mrs. Deegan angrily.

'Nothing at all my good woman,' said Macanasa, approaching her. 'Nothing at all, only ye better be careful of him. He's not right in the head, and he says queer things.'

'What queer things would he be saying?' said Mrs. Deegan.

'Well,' said Macanasa, 'he might be...' He paused and went over to Deegan. He put his hand on Deegan's shoulder. 'Was it about the cattle he was talking?' he whispered.

Deegan looked at his wife's face. It was rigid and fierce. Deegan, in response to this expression, suddenly became furious and jumped to his feet.

'You can go to hell, Paddy Macanasa,' he said, 'I'm not afeered of ye. I'll put my cattle on his land tomorrow with the dawn of the day.'

'And well ye might,' said Macanasa, stepping back. 'But there's a curse on that land, that'll lay low any grabber that puts his foot on it. It's foolish going against a curse.'

'We're not afraid of your curses,' cried Mrs. Deegan.

'Get out of my house,' yelled Deegan, making for the tongs.

The old couple had awakened and they were mumbling. The children were crying. The bitch was darting around the floor, her tail between her legs, barking.

Macanasa, moving towards the door, suddenly became excited and shouted: 'Look out now, ye scum,' he said. 'The Macanasas have power yet.'

Then, just as suddenly, his anger seemed to vanish. Opening the door, he turned, peered around the room, as if looking for something and then he opened his mouth wide and laughed outright. 'Sure don't take any harm out of what an old man says,' he whispered. 'I was only taking a rise outa ye. Send yer cattle in the morning and the good fairies'll take care of them. And if they don't I will. Goodnight now and God be with ye.'

He closed the door softly, coughed and trudged away up the yard noisily over the cobblestones.

The bitch began to whine uneasily.

CHAPTER VI

According to custom, Lawless fed at sunset in his yard. As in the morning he drank goat's milk and ate oaten cake. He also, at this meal, ate some sorrel leaves which grew profusely in the glen. Then he went into the house.

He brought his stool into the room where the human skull lay on the little table beside the votive lamp. He sat down facing the oil painting on the wall, to begin his daily contemplation. He was very excited.

He stared at the oil painting; but this night it did not arouse familiar thoughts in him. He had purchased it, after leaving jail, at a sales room on the Dublin quays, not for its commercial or artistic value (for it was fit only to be hung in some church as a representation of Jesus Christ in agony) but because it suggested to him the suffering of mankind. By contemplating the suffering of mankind he believed that his soul would become exalted and capable of abolishing that suffering. But, in a strange manner, this evening, even though he gazed at the horrible picture, it did not appear gruesome to him. Neither could his mind form any conception of human suffering. Suffering had become so remote from his consciousness that it was impossible to conceive it. Instead he could only think of the remarkable experiences he had had in the river; and the knowledge that his body was now the sanctuary of a divine influence.

'I can suffer no more,' he thought.

Thinking of this, his eyes wandered away from the picture and rested on the human skull, which lay on the table. That object, so terrifying to human beings, appeared to him now as commonplace and healthy as a stone or a blade of grass. Rather did it appear to him now as belonging to a form of life on a lower plane. He stretched out his two hands and touched its smooth, bony surface with his fingers; and he remembered the terror, now strange, with which he had first looked upon it; the difficulty of procuring it; the feeling of sacrilege with which he had given money to the dealer from whom he purchased it; the secrecy with which he had carried it off in a leather bag; the agony of the first night he had sat in front of it, contemplating death, that he might gain the power to end death. Now, of course, he was certain that there was no such thing, for him, as death. And he said, with tears in his eyes. 'Poor, ignorant, erring human skull! You once contained some mind that thought and thought in darkness and then dissolved into the earth from which it came; from darkness into darkness.'

He sat erect, rigid, on his stool and closed his eyes and then again his mind reverted to a conception of human suffering; for even though he himself was free from death by his conviction that he was immortal, he desired that all others should be equally so and their ignorance offended his happiness and made him unhappy with them. He shuddered and tried to flee from this thought, lest it might cast him down into an equal ignorance. He contemplated his body as he had done in the river. But no exaltation resulted. Instead a trivial thought entered his mind. He put his hand to his chin and said: 'I have forgotten to shave.'

He had until now been in the habit of shaving in the evening. That was of course while he conformed to social conventions; and as a habit is difficult to eradicate, although grown out of a totally different environment, he still shaved in the evening since his arrival in the glen. Now, however, he realised that his new discovery prevented his shaving himself any more. For, as his body was holy, it would be sacrilegious to run the risk of cutting it with a razor. It would be especially sacrilegious to offer it indignity by clipping the hairs that grew on it through the normal activity of its nature. Passing his fingers over his face, however, he felt the stubble of strong hair sprouting on it and he felt melancholy. He was cutting himself adrift completely from the conventions of his caste and from humanity. He felt lonely; more lonely than he had ever felt in his life. And for a moment he shrank in fear from the implications of his holiness. A temptation assailed him again, to flee downwards, away from the pursuit of godliness.

He arose slowly and then stood still trying to arrest his thoughts. He felt the unknown quality in his body diminishing until it became a single point and almost vanished. Suddenly, with great force, he clasped his arms across his chest. A haze passed before his eyes. His doubts vanished and he felt the mysterious quality expand again and take possession of his being. Again, as in the river, it seemed that his body became much larger, lighter, practically without weight. With his arms folded he turned about and took several paces forward towards the window. His legs trembled as he walked.

He looked from the window and listened to the murmuring of the birds. A strange excitement, which he had never before experienced now possessed him. His personality was changing completely without any apparent warning. Through the amazing lucidity which was now a characteristic of his intelligence, he could watch this change, as if it were taking place in some person other than himself. He could feel a new powerful personality coming into him and his own personality dissolving. He thought with extraordinary rapidity and ease. He kept shuddering with relief; for it appeared that he had been all his conscious life standing on the brink of a precipice, which he had now escaped by becoming endowed with a quality of buoyancy. The blindness which formerly enveloped his mind had now given way to a joyous certainty.

His mind soared over the earth, and he contemplated all humanity striving beneath him. He saw them fall, die, become mangled, wasted by disease, laugh, sing, curse, cry in anguish, moving in hordes anxiously, halting for generations in great cities. And he understood the purpose of their movements. And he no longer experienced any partiality towards any section of them. He no longer differentiated between their acts for their morality had ceased to have any meaning for him. It was apparent that all their acts were performed towards the one end and that murder, war, famine, lust, pestilence, greed, lechery, love, benevolence, valour, cowardice and blasphemy were all manifestations of the struggle for the quality which he himself now possessed; the immortality that is the property of godliness.

He clenched his fists and spread his arms out mightily from his shoulders and opening wide his palms, he wished to cover all humanity beneath their holy shelter and dispel the darkness that overshadowed their groping minds. His mind exulted. At last it was clear he need not fear to call others to his state, since he was purified. His face shone with a divine light, and he murmured: 'Fear is dead and hatred and with them death. I fear no more. At last all fear shall cease. What sign shall I give them?'

He began to wonder, for although he could see humanity struggling for the knowledge he possessed he did not know how he had come into the possession of this knowledge and therefore could not impart it.

He moved away from the window and falling into a trance he began to pick books from the shelves and open the pages. It was some time before he was aware of what he was doing, and when he became aware of it, he smiled and dropped the book he held. He surveyed the rows of books and shook his head. How futile they were! Scores and scores of books about religion, and in all of them there was not one atom of knowledge, other than foolish conjecture.

'This is queer,' he thought. 'I now know everything and yet what I know has no language. I cannot express it. How can I tell them?' He mused and then he thought: 'The same power that entered me shall enter them through me without words.'

Unable to keep still, owing to the excitement of his nerves, he wandered about from room to room. Then he lay down on his bed, but he could not rest. He got up again and walked around. He was still in a thoughtless trance, and in this state his normal instincts again took control of his body.

I must go out for a walk,' he thought. 'The fresh air will do me good.'

He was going out the door into the yard when he noticed a figure at the gate. The gate creaked and opened. Old Macanasa entered the yard. Lawless stood still. His face, still illuminated by an ecstatic smile, became transfixed and then the smile vanished slowly, giving way to an expression of wonder and then of pain. Macanasa approached slowly without speaking. The two goats, which had been standing side by side on the roof of the shed to the right of the house, began to snort and to beat the corrugated iron roof sharply with their hoofs. When Macanasa was within a few feet of Lawless, he halted, leaned both hands on his stick and said: 'God save all here. It's a fine night.'

Lawless tried to answer but a curious feeling of wonder prevented him from articulating the words. Should he stretch out his right hand and give a blessing, to see if .... ? He did not do so, for he began to wonder why his body seemed to contract and to sink down.

Macanasa came a pace nearer and said, with his foot on the iron foot wiper that lay in front of the door: 'I said I'd come at night.'

'Yes?' said Lawless with a start. Just then remembering Macanasa's visit that morning.

'At night,' said Macanasa. 'There do be a power of strange things moving about at night. But ye have to belong to the place to be able to see them or else to be a very holy man, same as yer honour.'

'He tempts me,' thought Lawless.

'Who is he?' He remained silent.

Macanasa coughed. 'They carried off Bridget Macanasa,' he whispered, 'her that lived here before you came.'

'How do you mean?' said Lawless, aloud. 'Who carried her off?' Might there be another force? he wondered. All things had their source, both good and evil. Man had known that for thousands of years.

'She was buried in the graveyard,' said Macanasa, 'but I know it wasn't herself was buried. She was gone before she died. Swept away.' He made a gesture. 'There's more living things that we can't see than what we can see,' he continued, mysteriously.

Lawless moved forward and touched the old man on the shoulder. 'Come, tell me what you mean.'

'Sit down here,' whispered Macanasa 'and listen to them birds flying.'

They sat down side by side on the doorstep.

'Now listen,' said Macanasa.

They both listened. At first there was an eerie silence. In front, through the gaps between the tree branches, they saw the mountain rise before them dark grey and shadowy and silent. Afar off, made distant by the night, the stark shapes of tall trees stood out on the mountain tops; and above them the blue sky was dappled with pale stars. The sky looked cold.

Then they heard the whirring sound of birds' wings. No bird was visible and the sounds were mysterious, high up in the firmament, a powerful flapping of wings, passing rapidly. Then at a distance, on the ground, another bird made a chirping sound; and, as if in answer, a vigorous wheezing sound arose elsewhere, like the sound of a pump, again there was silence.

Listening, Lawless now found that the silence was full of sound. Gazing intently, the form of the earth assumed strange shapes in his eyes. He felt that something evil was at hand. He looked at Macanasa's face. The face was close to his and perfectly motionless. The old man's mouth was shut tightly. His queer features were without life and the raised chin exposed the hollow neck that had a deep hole beside the windpipe. But his eyes were transformed. There was a wild, mystic look in them; as if they were communing with something unseen.

'Who is he?' thought Lawless again.

Macanasa thrust out his hand and gripped Lawless's knee. His eyes shone. 'Did ye hear anything?'

'Birds.'

'Did ye see anything?'

'I saw the mountain and the trees.'

'Is that all?'

'What should I see?'

'The dead travelling in the night.'

'What dead?'

'The Macanasas.' The old man gripped the knee tighter and whispered in a hoarse voice.

'They do be guarding the land, since the foreigners came over the mountains and killed them with their swords. And long ago, there were other laws here and people didn't believe what they do now. And there are things here,' he pushed his face towards Lawless's and cried in a powerful voice, 'that we can't talk about for fear of the priests. There's a little raheen behind the house,' continued Macanasa. 'It's that place in the fields where ye see the dead wood fallen among the trees. There are fairies living there, and if you take any of that wood some evil'll fall on ye. They do be guarding the land.'

'Have you seen them?' asked Lawless, coldly.

'Eh?' The old man feigned deafness.

'Have you seen them?' repeated Lawless.

'Only fools see with their eyes,' murmured the old man. 'But the wise man sees with his mind.'

'I see,' said Lawless.

'What d'ye see?' said Macanasa in a loud tone.

They both got to their feet. They faced one another.

'This morning I feared you,' said Lawless. 'But you no longer hold any power over my soul. Bow down before me, purify yourself of greed and you, too, shall understand good instead of evil.'

Macanasa took a pace backwards and spat upon his stick. An ugly look came into his eyes. Lawless watched him calmly.

Suddenly Macanasa muttered something and turned. He walked away several paces. Then he halted and turned again. He came forward slowly until he was beside Lawless. 'Ye don't believe what I said?' he whispered.

Lawless did not speak.

'But ye will soon,' said Macanasa, raising his stick in a menacing fashion. 'Ye will soon, for I see a dark shadow on yer house.'

With that he shuffled off out of the gate. Lawless did not move until the old man had disappeared. Then he himself also passed out the gate, crossed the stream and mounted the great rock. He looked at the sky. The sky was full of stars. A cool breeze blew fitfully making no sound. A horse neighed.

A pale yellow light sped down the glen and a large moon appeared over a mountain top.

CHAPTER VII

The young men of the neighbourhood had gathered in Mrs. Dillon's cottage. Although none of them was aware of it, they had all come in pursuit of Mrs. Dillon. She was the only attractive young woman in that part of the glen; and being married to a degenerate husband who maintained her in dire poverty, her restless soul vented its spleen on society by arousing the passions of all the males in her environment. The result was that she and her husband were most unhappy mates; their house was in a filthy, ramshackle condition; their land was becoming barren; and their two children were unhealthy. Around the house there was mud, ruin and desolation, so that even their little group of tall trees looked weary of this desolate environment and their nether branches fell one by one, leaving naked trunks, capped on high by tufts of leafy twigs.

Like birds of prey that hover about a dying animal, it is invariably the custom in remote Irish villages for the young men to make such a withering household their meeting place. In our remote villages, where morals are so primitively strict and the father still uses the thong to correct the least fault in conduct, young men seek such a house that is divided against itself, in order to relax and make merry and perhaps pluck an unprotected fruit.

That night there was a larger gathering than usual in Mrs. Dillon's kitchen; because Myles Cronin, the accordion player, had just come home on furlough from the Army, and people had gathered to hear him play. He was sitting in the corner seat of the hearth, with his legs crossed, smoking a cigarette while he played the instrument. He had a girlish red face that looked strangely sophisticated compared to the other faces in the room. Three of Macanasa's sons were there also, all sitting side by side on one long form. They were all tall, lean, long nosed, with cunning eyes and gentle mouths. The oldest was forty years of age, and the youngest was thirty; but they were all unmarried. The youngest son was not there, because he was an epileptic, who hardly ever left home and then only in daytime.

There were three other young men, two of them married peasants and the third a large farm labourer from a small estate beyond the opposite mountain. There was also a very old man from across the river, a relative of Mrs. Dillon's. He always came in the hope of getting tobacco from the young men.

Opposite the soldier who played the accordion Larry Dillon was sitting, nursing his two children. One child of eighteen months was on his knee and the other child of three years sat on the hearthstones with his thumb in his mouth, motionless and silent. The father's face was like the children's faces, timid, weak, dirty. He had not shaved for many days, because during the previous week, while quarrelling with his wife through jealousy, he had cut her finger with a razor he was using at the time, by accident. Thereupon, in terror, he had thrown away the razor and determined to shave no more. His ragged clothes and sullen demeanour were shocking to behold.

The pity that such a spectacle aroused was an acute pain; because one could see, beneath the depravity, gentleness that might have borne good fruit in different circumstances. The man seemed destined by nature for the avocation of a humble, industrious clerk, or some such profession of the weak and characterless; those who bow when kicked and are guided in their every act by a rigid code of behaviour; but who, if they miss their tide, are pimps, currish beggars and half-witted louts. They are as incapable of great evil as of great virtue. They are the scourings of nature's womb, and she crushes them mercilessly.

Yet this strange weakling was gentle and kind to animals and children. And he would watch, with open lips and wondering eyes, the stars at night or listen rapturously to the murmur of the river on a summer's day, dreaming of some beauty which his thoughtless mind could not envisage.

Although it was long past milking time, the cows had just been milked and Mrs. Dillon was at a table straining the milk. While she was doing so, she kept fidgeting about, talking in spite of the music, spilling the milk on the floor in her excitement, kicking the collie dog that tried to drink the spilt milk and eating lozenges out of a paper bag which lay in the pocket of her apron.

Secretly, the eyes of all the young men watched her. Secretly her husband's timid eyes watched the watching eyes of the young men. And, conscious of all this watching, her black eyes flashed. Smiles, frowns and gleams of intelligence flashed across her passionate beautiful countenance. In the dim light of the lamp her slim, graceful body had an elfin charm. In spite of her shabby clothes, there was a queenly grace in her movements; and even her bedraggled black hair was a glorious crown on such a comely head. But what a disturbing influence! How impossible to imprison in an embrace that subtle, dancing figure!

The music stopped. She leaned against the table and wiped her thin arm across her brow.

'God! Ye make me sad, Myles,' she said, 'playing that tune. Reminds me when I was working in a hotel in Dublin. The nights I used to have.'

Nobody replied.

'Play another tune, Myles,' said Larry Dillon.

The soldier did not reply, but putting down his instrument, he relit his cigarette from an ember of the fire.

'The glen is dead,' said the old man, 'and it's for want of women.'

They all laughed.

'It's for want of men,' said Mrs. Dillon in a low voice.

'It's for want of money,' said one of the Macanasas.

'And I a young lad,' continued the old man, 'there used to be dances at Tierney's Cross every Sunday night. Lashings of young girls; fine strapping girls as big as – as big as cows.'

All the young men laughed again.

'It's the truth I'm telling ye,' said the old man seriously. 'As big as cows they were.'

'I wish I was a thousand miles away from it,' said Mrs. Dillon in a fierce whisper. 'I hate this place.'

'Well,' said the eldest Macanasa slowly, 'there's a lot of people coming into it since the war.'

'I wish them luck,' said Mrs. Dillon. 'I wish they bought this place from Larry. I'm always asking him to take me to America.'

'Fifty years ago,' said the old man, 'in this house I'm sitting in, there was dead meat hanging from the roof, so thick ye couldn't see a rafter.'

Mrs. Dillon wiped the table with a rag and then sat on the edge of the table, dangling her legs. She adjusted the hooks at the waist of her skirt. All the young men watched. There was a silence. The soldier played a bar and then began to fiddle with a key that was broken.

'Still it's a poor thing to leave the place where ye were born,' said Macanasa's second son.

'So it is,' said Macanasa's third son. 'It's hard work foraging on another man's share and it's a shame to let the foreigner sit on yer hearthstone.'

'God! There are queer people coming here right enough,' said Mrs. Dillon. 'That Dr. Stevens is a queer man. The way he watches ye with his little eyes. I'm afraid of me life of him.'

'He has great learning,' said the old man.

'He can take his learning somewhere else,' said Macanasa's third son. 'We could do without him.'

'I wouldn't care to meet him on a dark night,' said Mrs. Dillon. 'These quiet people are the worst.'

'And where would you be meeting him on a dark night?' said Larry Dillon. 'Sure he is not a night walker.'

'Mind yer business,' said she sharply. 'The way he looked at me today by the river. His eyes go through ye. I tell ye it's want of men is the matter with this glen. There's no spunk in the men that's left.' She passed rapidly across the floor to the lamp and lowered the wick. All eyes followed her movements. 'Men like that big brute Deegan. His wife is in the family way again. Trying to put his arms around me coming up in the cart from the village and his wife sitting the other side of him. She hasn't spoken to me since.'

The young men laughed uneasily. They looked furtively at one another.

'They say that Mr. Lawless is queer in the head,' said the old man.

'Police are after him,' said the soldier laconically.

'Ha, ha,' all said, looking towards the soldier.

'Yep,' said the soldier, with an air of importance. 'He's one o' these bank robbers or communists, or whatever ye call them. We got his number. Locked up a few times. Let off again. Influence. Government keeping an eye on him.' He spat into the fire. 'Wouldn't surprise me, any day, see him on the carpet again, locked up, term of his natural.

Should be bloody well creased, all these revolution fellahs. Knocked on the nozzle.'

They were all impressed by the soldier's speech. The soldier stuck out his chest, ran his fingers up and down the keys a few times, played a bar and then stopped again.

'Well,' said the old man, 'I don't know what to say. He acts queer.'

'His goats is queer,' said another.

'Well, he has lovely eyes, anyway,' said Mrs. Dillon. 'And his hands are so white. I'd love to shake hands with him, to touch his hands.'

'Lots o' them fellahs,' said the soldier 'are landlords' sons, fired out, burned, plugged – 'em don't know what to do with themselves. Some gone balmy, some start stunts like this fellah, gamin' on wanting to free the country. Put them under a headstone. That's what I say.'

'He told my father that nobody was going to die no more,' said the oldest of Macanasa's sons.

Everybody laughed except the old man, Larry Dillon and the soldier.

'That's a soft bar,' said the soldier.

'It's not right to laugh,' said the old man. 'That's the sin agin the Holy Ghost. Every man has to be ready when the Lord calls him.'

'Even the crows die,' said Larry Dillon in his childish voice.

'Old soldiers never die,' said the soldier.

'God! I'd hate to live for ever,' said Mrs. Dillon. 'Wouldn't it be awful to live for a thousand years in this glen?'

'Be all right at Monte Carlo,' said the soldier.

'I heard Dr. Stevens say,' murmured the oldest of Macanasa's sons, 'that there are more suns than one, and that the moon was alive once.'

'God between us and harm,' said the old man. 'Them learned men are pulling the roof of Heaven down over our heads. It's not safe for the larks nowadays. Couldn't they leave the world as it was, so that the dead could rest and the living could die in peace?'

'All them fellahs are balmy,' said the soldier. 'We can make bombs now in the Army ud blow this bloody glen into atoms. Aye, and that bloody doctor along with it. Poison gas out of an aeroplane. Kill every rabbit in this glen down in his hole. All a damn cod, nobody going to die no more. More like it, nobody going to live no more shortly. That fellah's going to get the term of his natural. Police after him. Stirring up the people.'

'I hate that Dr. Stevens,' said Mrs. Dillon, moving towards the door of the bedroom at the left of the kitchen.

All eyes followed her into the bedroom. They became silent waiting for her re-appearance. She had put a shawl about her shoulders.

'I'm going down the road to Mrs. Burke's,' she said to her husband. 'I won't be a minute.'

'What's taking ye out at this hour o' the night?' said her husband.

'Castor oil for Barney,' she said.

'Wasn't it yesterday ye got it in the village?' he said suspiciously.

She paused and scolded him furiously. She banged the door after her. Outside the fence of the yard she took a full bottle of castor oil from her shawl and put it in a hole in the fence. Then her face brightened. It became eager. She began to walk rapidly almost running, along the path towards the red-roofed house.

There was a bright moon that made her slim figure distinct against the horizon. Her figure passed through a gap into a field to the right. It became blurred as it dipped into a hollow that was overgrown with briars and ferns. It moved on slowly until it reached a large mound of stones that was surrounded with bushes. There it halted.

Then another figure appeared from in front and approached slowly. Both figures spoke. They talked for a while. Then her figure fled, uttering a little cry. The strange figure pursued her. The strange figure caught her. There was the sound of a kiss. Then she broke loose panting.

'I hate you' she hissed. 'I hate you, with your little eyes. He has got lovely eyes and white long hands. That's the man I'd like to cuddle.'

She laughed and fled.

CHAPTER VIII

The priests of the parish hardly ever visited the glen, except on urgent duty or to collect their special dues. These special dues, collected by the curate, were formerly called 'Oats Money,' in the days when a country priest kept a horse to visit his parishioners. Now the title of this money tribute has been changed to 'Petrol Money', in certain parts, owing to the advance of science and the general overthrow of the horse by the motor car. Previous to the collection of dues of any sort, it is usual for priests to lecture their congregations on the terrors of hell and on the awful punishment that awaits those who do not give proper financial support to their religious masters.

On the Sunday following the events just related, the curate of the parish preached an especially horrifying sermon. He had, of course, heard of Lawless's strange conduct and the disturbance caused by his appearance among the glen dwellers. The other intellectuals, living in the glen before Lawless, had not given the priest any cause for alarm, because, even though they lived the lives of pagans, they were all Protestants and therefore outside the priest's jurisdiction. He used them as a warning to those of his own sect, outside of which there was no hope of leading a moral life. Lawless, however, even though he was by birth a Protestant, was reputed to be trying to proselytise the people by preaching strange doctrines. The priest determined to 'scotch the heretical snake' and to warn the people at the same time that 'Petrol Money' must be paid generously.

As the Sunday was fine, almost every parishioner appeared at Mass. The chapel was crowded. When the priest took off his outer vestments at the altar and turned around to preach, the people knew by the expression on his face that something terrible was about to be announced. Those who had been unable to gain admission owing to the crowd now pressed into the open doorway, so that the air was stifling.

The priest, by name Eugene Raverty, was an extraordinary person. Though still merely twenty-eight years of age, a fanatical and morbid conscience had darkened his countenance, giving it the appearance of unhappy old age. He had forbidding black eyes. Black eyes are generally large and bovine. But his were small, imbued with a certain subtlety of expression impossible to describe. At first they inspired disgust; but almost immediately a curious sensation of pity followed. Not pity for the priest himself, but for the eyes, which had a personality of their own. They were like a survival of some remotely primitive being that had been planted in the priest's head. They were intent with awful fear and awful brutality, united with the childish simplicity that is the peculiar quality of the aboriginal. They did not blink; but periodically, as if dragged down by tortuous thoughts, the heavy black brows descended over them. Then their balls glistened.

He had a tall, awkward figure, not heavy, but remarkably bony. His stout jaws already seemed, at a distance, covered with a thick growth of dark beard; even when smoothly shaven one could see, when close, the dark roots of the hair on the sallow skin.

After reading the gospel for the Sunday, he evidently experienced great difficulty in beginning his sermon. He stood at the altar in silence, staring fiercely in front of him, motionless. There was utter silence in the church. The still summer day became heavy with suppressed sound, as if the very air heaved up in a compact mass against the stained glass windows and the whitewashed walls, to listen to the denunciation of immorality and heresy about to be made by the representative, on this terrestrial globe, of the Creator of the universe. Then the priest's knees began to tremble, slightly swaying the loose folds of the white alb that covered them. Then his right hand shot out and he opened his lips. He gave voice to these words.

'Hell!' he cried in a thundering voice that was hoarse with the fury of fanaticism. 'What is hell?'

There was no reply from the congregation, but several murmured something, and others struck their breasts fervently.

'Hell,' continued the priest, answering on his own account, 'is so terrible that the human mind can form no conception of its horror. Picture to yourselves all the coal in the world, millions of tons of coal, collected in one heap and set on fire, until the roar of the flames was greater than the mightiest thunder, and then millions of gallons of petrol thrown on top of it, until the flames, rising into the air, reached the highest clouds, so hot that the ocean would be dried up, and then, you have no conception of hell. Hell is far worse than that. Hell is slow torture. I can't tell you what hell is like. Because if I did, every one in this church would die of fright. The very mention of its horrors would cause the earth to open up and swallow us all, down, down into the pit of hell.'

The priest gasped and drew a deep breath. Already, owing to the stifling air and the ferocity of his passion, beads of perspiration stood out on his face. The brows swooped down over his glistening black eyes, and his jaws trembled. He surveyed his audience eagerly like a great dog whose thunderous barking has hypnotised a herd of sheep. The audience gaped, wild-eyed, yet ecstatic with a certain perverted joy at the horrors that were in store for them. Their bodies swayed slightly. With a start, as of a runner about to plunge forward, the priest continued:

'And what price does the devil pay you in return for the everlasting damnation of your souls? What price? What joy, what happiness do you get in return for being damned and burned and roasted alive for millions and billions of years, tormented with thirst, hunger and most horrible diseases, plunged in everlasting darkness, in silence, in terrible silence, with the Eye of God ever staring down into the bottomless pit upon you, accusing you with pointed finger and that terrible Voice for ever in your ears: 'Depart from me, ye accursed, into the everlasting flames of hell'? Oh, my brethren, ye should demand a great, great price from the tempter before ye succumb to his cunning voice and to the lascivious touch of his slimy body. But no! Your price is small, very small. For one word of blasphemy against God the Father, against the Divine Saviour, against Holy Mother Church, against the Mother of God, the pit is opened, gaping, ready to devour you; and were it not for the mercy of God, through his intermediaries, the priests in the confessional, that pit would swallow you after one fall. One moment of doubt, one weak moment during which you listen to the voice of the atheist, the socialist, the heretic, that is the price you get. And worse still, the worst of all sins, the sin of the flesh, the sin of slime and ugliness, no matter how it is robed in purple and fine linen, scented with the perfumes of the East and glorified by heathen poetry, that sin that cried out to the Blessed Mother for vengeance, the sin of lust and incontinence.'

Here the priest gasped again. He was now bathed in perspiration. Under his armpits the perspiration oozed through the white alb, discolouring the linen. The audience, however, was now intent. It no longer swayed. There was an eager look in the faces of the people.

'A few moments of false pleasure,' whispered the priest. 'Just the tingling of a nerve, and two souls are damned.'

He paused again. The people were amazed at his daring, and for a few moments it appeared that the spell of terror was broken, by the angry look that came into the faces of the respectable people from the village. But the priest went on hurriedly, and the situation was saved.

'There are women in this congregation,' cried the priest in a loud voice, 'straight on the road to hell, and if they do not beware in time, I will denounce them from this altar; I will denounce them in the highways and the lanes where they seek their companions in sin. I am going to put a stop to vice in this parish. Aye, and I'm going to root out heresy and paganism wherever it shows its foul head. I have not spoken of this until now, but I have been for a long time aware of what is happening in a certain part of this parish. We are honoured, in a certain part of the parish, by the company of fools that pose as artists and intellectual sophists, scientists, and what not. The wave of irreligion, revolution and debauchery that is trying to overwhelm the world in sensualism and sin has stuck one of its foul claws into this holy parish. But I'm going to cut that claw; even though it masquerades under the guise of Anti-Christ. For, at the bottom of all these false preachers and artists and intellectuals, when the false trappings of learning and idealism are cut away, there remains only the lust of the flesh and the concupiscence of the spirit. Tomorrow I'm going to go the rounds of the parish to collect the yearly dues of the curate, and I'll give particular attention to this matter. And in that certain part of the parish I'll keep my eyes and ears open, and I shall not spare. I shall not spare,' he concluded, 'either man or woman, for severity is necessary, when hell is gaping and Lucifer is sharpening his prongs for falling souls.'

With that he turned about, exhausted, and pulled his vestments over his head. Several old people threw themselves prostrate and struck the floor violently with their foreheads.

Mrs. Dillon, sitting at the back of the church, went on her knees and bit the knuckles of her hand. Her eyes were blazing with anger.

CHAPTER IX

While the priest was delivering his sermon, a very interesting scene was being enacted in the glen. Following Lawless's instructions, the Deegans had put their horses on Lawless's land. The Dillons, anxious to avail themselves of the same privilege, asked Lawless's permission to put their cattle on the land. Lawless gave them permission. Forthwith Dillon, who had only one horse, put his horse, cows and sheep to graze on the land. The Deegans responded by putting their cows and sheep in with their horses. The Macanasas, enraged at what was taking place and being unable to prevent it at the moment, brought across the river a small herd of black mountain bullocks which they were trying to fatten for the market. All these animals joined together in a great mass on the marshland in front of the red-roofed house. There was a great bellowing, bleating and neighing, while some of the beasts, afraid of the great crowd in which they suddenly found themselves, lost their senses and began to fight, kick and gore one another.

Whatever advantage the people gained by the free grazing was lost through the time and energy they spent looking after their cattle. The Macanasas kept moving about, threatening; while the other two families were also busy, separating contending beasts and watching the Macanasas. They even kept watch all night, lest the Macanasas might raid the herd under cover of darkness. This lasted for three days.

During that time nobody saw Lawless, for he remained indoors. Miss Hopkins, an eccentric old maid, called on him on Saturday, but she was unable to gain admission to the house. The goats roamed about the yard all the time, apparently in a disturbed state, but they must have been attended to regularly, because their udders were noticed to be slack during the course of each day.

Dr. Stevens alone appeared to be amused by the disturbance about the cattle. He spent most of the time watching the quarrels of the people, sitting on a fence near the red-roofed house. Or, indeed, he may have been waiting for Lawless's appearance.

Then on Sunday morning everybody went to Mass, except Lawless and Dr. Stevens. Even the old maid went to Mass. She was not a Catholic, and her own peculiar religion was not yet registered as an orthodox creed; but perhaps she went for the sake of the walk across the river and up the mountain; or because her interest in folk magic brought her.

When everything was quiet, Macanasa crossed the river with two dogs, one a large collie, and the other a malicious half-breed of a reddish colour, a large fellow with curved tangs on his hind legs. He took cover behind the boundary fence dividing his land from Lawless's land, at a point where the broad stretch of marshland lay in front of him. Owing to the heat of the day, all the beasts had gathered about a spring a short distance to the front of the house and a little to the right. The sheep, in three herds, were lying above the beasts among the furze bushes. All the beasts were quiet.

Then Macanasa brought his two dogs to a break in the fence and held them close together for some time, pointing to the cattle and muttering something. Suddenly he loosed the collie. Uttering a low cry, the collie dashed forward, running sideways. The mongrel also tried to dash forward, but Macanasa held the brute by the ears, shaking him, until the animal was distraught with rage and slavered at the mouth. Then he loosed him also. The mongrel uttered a single yell, hurled himself forward and struck the ground with his chest. He rose again, and whining as if in close pursuit of prey, he flew after the collie bitch.

Macanasa lowered his head and hurried away back towards the river, stooping under cover of the fences. When he reached the river bank he turned to the left and walked rapidly until he reached a little bay that was lined with pebbles. There he sat on a rock, took off his shoes and socks and bathed his feet in the running water. Then he stretched out flat on the pebbles, with his belly to the sun and his hat covering his face. He seemed to have fallen asleep.

In the meantime the dogs were active. First they concentrated on the horses, separated Macanasa's horses from the others and drove the others up the mountainside, barking loudly. A roan gelding belonging to Deegan at first attacked the dogs, but finding the mares in mad flight the gelding turned tail and pursued them. Then the dogs drove the cows up the mountainside. It was more difficult to rout the cows, as the clumsy beasts hurtled about trying to gore the dogs. But the very effort of pursuing the dogs maddened the cows. They also went into a panic and fled. Already irritated by the summer heat, the excitement gave them summer fever. They raised their tails, lowered their heads and galloped away aimlessly, moaning helplessly when the dogs bit at their thighs or flanks.

All the while, Macanasa's bullocks stood in a compact mass, watching the dogs.

Just as the dogs were about to attack the sheep, Lawless appeared from his house at a run. He had been startled by the neighing, bellowing, lowing, yapping, bleating and snorting; a medley of sound that was truly horrible to hear. Seeing the dogs harrying the animals, he ran out the gate and as he was crossing the stream he stooped and picked up two small stones. Holding the stones, one in each hand, he continued to run. But he had not gone far when he halted with a start and looked at the stones.

He undoubtedly was very ill. Through the thick growth of hair on his unshaven face, the skin was pallid and drawn. The eyes were bloodshot and the nostrils had that peculiarly strained appearance which is always a sign of illness in highly strung individuals. He appeared also to have grown a great deal thinner during the past few days. But what was most strange was his countenance. The calm, gentle look had disappeared. And in its place there was a tortured expression, seen only in the faces of those who are enduring the agonies of despair. Yet, even now, the face was not harsh or crude. But its very refinement made the despair still more obvious.

He looked at the stones he held, wondering why he had picked them up. Then the dogs, now chasing the sheep, ran across the marsh in front of him. Without thinking, he ran after them, crying out angrily and hurling the stones. One of the stones hit the collie bitch on the side and knocked her down. She screamed with pain, jumped to her feet and fled with her tail between her legs, without even troubling to look at the man that had thrown the stone. The other dog ran on, but finding himself alone, he also turned around shortly and saw Lawless. He stopped running, growled and trotted off slowly homeward, with his tail half raised and his mane erect, licking his jaws with his red tongue. The startled sheep kept running on straight ahead until they passed over the brows of the moor, going goodness knows whither.

All the other cattle, except Macanasa's had already passed out of sight, jumping fences and ditches, in mad flight, away through the glen.

Lawless began to walk down slowly towards his house. Three people were approaching him from that direction. They were Larry Dillon, grandfather Deegan and Dr. Stevens. Dillon had been left at home to look after the children. He had one child on his shoulder and he was leading the other by the hand. Grandfather Deegan had his hat in his hand and he was already exhausted. Dr. Stevens was coming up slowly behind him. He carried a fishing rod, which he had been using on the river when he heard the quarrel.

'Whose dogs are those?' said Lawless to Dillon.

Dillon was so amazed at Lawless's voice that he took the child from his shoulder and put it on the ground. He did not reply. Lawless had spoken in a loud, angry, commanding voice, entirely different from the meek tones previously characteristic of him.

'Whose dogs are those, I say?' he cried once more, still approaching.

'Macanasa's dogs sir,' said Dillon.

The old man came up with his left hand to his hat. 'At the hour of Mass he did it, the ruffian.'

Lawless looked sharply at him. 'You are all fools, and I am a fool to take any interest in you. Damn you all. I've been a fool all my life. Go now. Collect your animals and take them to the devil out of my sight. Be off. Go now.'

The two peasants looked at him suspiciously and did not move. He came forward suddenly. Then they went off after the cattle.

'What has happened?' said Dr. Stevens in his indolent voice.

Lawless had not seen Dr. Stevens until then. He looked at him curiously. 'Good morning.'

Stevens nodded his head and looked closely at Lawless. Lawless met the other's eyes arrogantly, yet with no appearance of remembering that he had ever seen the man before. Indifferently, in fact, as he had looked at the peasants.

'Excuse me,' said Stevens, 'but you look ill. Could I help in any way? I'm a doctor.'

'Doctor!' A smile distorted Lawless's face. 'How ridiculous! '

Stevens laughed soundlessly and without humour. 'I'm sorry, but here in the wilds...'

'Never mind,' said Lawless, 'come and talk to me. Human beings doctor one another in that way. Two sheep in a storm. Come into the house, will you?'

They crossed the stream and entered the yard. Lawless walked furiously but without making much headway and his gait was unsteady. Stevens, following slowly, studied him closely and thought: 'This is probably his normal state. Something must have happened.'

At the door of the house, Lawless turned: 'There is only one seat.'

'Why not sit out here?'

'No, no,' said Lawless. 'Come inside, I feel menaced by the...' He did not finish the sentence, but waved his hand and went indoors. Stevens followed him. Lawless sat down on the stool in the centre of the floor. He had obviously been sitting there for a long time because there were bread crumbs, milk stains and other slight refuse on the floor about the stool. The whole room looked much dirtier than it had been a few days previously. There was, too, something degrading about it.

Stevens leaned his fishing rod against the wall of the house, took a small white lozenge from a packet, put the lozenge in his mouth, coughed, wiped his hands with a handkerchief and entered the house. Without seeming to look at anything, he walked casually a little distance forward and then turned slowly to the left, touched the window sill with the tips of his fingers and sat down languidly on the edge of it. But even though he had not seemed to look, his little eyes had made furtive rushes in all directions. They noted every detail, politely and, as it were, without giving offence.

Lawless stared at him bluntly. Lawless's eyes saw nothing physical. The brilliant discs struggled violently for a glimpse of an invisible soul which they tried to envisage. 'What are you doing here?' he said at length.

'I think I told you that I......'

'When? What did you tell me?'

'Don't you remember the other day down by the river, you met me...'

'Oh, yes,' said Lawless, striking his head. 'I remember. You were saying that you...'

'Well, I don't think I told you exactly what I was here for. In fact, I couldn't really tell you, because I'm still in the experimental stage. But I have made rather interesting observations, and also established a theory.'

While Stevens was speaking, Lawless seemed to have lost all interest, as if the man were a trivial fellow, to whose conversation one might listen merely for the sake of politeness. 'Let's come to the point,' he said quickly. 'What do you believe?'

'You want to talk about that? It's very difficult to answer. Words are misleading and anyway I don't suppose we'd understand one another.'

'I mean generally,' said Lawless. 'What is your general attitude towards life. I'm not suffering from broken bones. It's something else. You say you are a doctor. But the help I need is the help one animal gives to another, nearness and something.... What do we make of that storm? It's knocked us down, at least me. Who sent it? Why did we not foresee it? How can we escape?'

Stevens shook his head slowly and his little eyes opened wide. 'What the devil is he talking about now?' he thought.

'Well?' said Lawless.

'I don't quite understand. Anything I can do of course, I'm only too willing.'

'Well. What is your attitude towards this THING,' he struck his chest, 'life and the object of it, the end, the ultimate purpose of it?'

'Ah! You told me, I think, that you were here to find God.'

'Answer my question. Then we can discuss and perhaps two souls shuddering together, facing the storm, may find a sheltered cave.'

'I suppose you mean, do I believe in God?'

'Yes. Just that, more or less, though not quite.'

'I don't know really.'

'Do you believe in anything?'

'I don't know.'

'Yes... just now I too am in that position. I don't know... anything.' Lawless made movements with his head, lips and fingers as if he were counting figures rapidly.

'Not knowing anything,' continued Stevens calmly, 'seems to me to be the normal condition of a reasoning mind. We seek but we seem to move along a chain of knowledge, catching link after link, only to find there is another ahead, dimly ahead. In fact, it's paradoxical. The more we know the less we know, because each new discovery gives birth to several new...'

'All that is sophistry. I also am clever at words. If you know nothing,' said Lawless with an air of authority, 'you can't know that some don't know everything.'

'Yes,' said Stevens with a slight bow.

'But what is extraordinary,' continued Lawless in a calmer tone... He appeared to be satisfied at his own cleverness. 'What is extraordinary is that you and I should arrive at the same conclusion by opposite methods. I seeking God. You seeking the devil. You are the type I have always detested. The agnostic philosopher. You are always scratching at the surface of life and then cocking your head wisely to one side and cackling. You are all, all you fellows, like hens in a barnyard. Scratch, scratch, but you never lay an egg. And your cackle is mistaken for wisdom. You sneer but you do not create. No, sir. The great wave of life rushes past you, the vast horde of humanity struggling to find a meaning for existence, struggling to batter down the gate of Heaven with their hands, and you stand aside, shrugging your shoulders, watching the contortions of the bodies, careless and contemptuous of the one beautiful thing, the soul of man struggling towards the light. Yes. That one thing I know as certain. The mission of man is to open the gate of Heaven.' Lawless opened out his arms and sat that way as if he were pointing out the way to Heaven.

'Quite,' said Stevens. 'I quite agree with you.' He coughed and he thought 'It's best to agree with him.' Then he became irritated, rubbed his nose and said: 'But this human horde you speak of – it must be fed. Its life must be preserved. Frankly I'm more interested in life than in Heaven. And you must admit that scientists and agnostic philosophers, as you call them, have done more.... done more to prolong life, make it comfortable, make beauty possible...'

'Beauty!' interjected Lawless.

'Yes, beauty,' said Stevens 'than – than the God-seeking horde or its leaders. And I don't believe the human horde seeks God, not in your sense...' He stopped suddenly.

'Go on,' said Lawless, smiling. 'I'm listening. Your scepticism is vanishing. You have become dogmatic, in fact.'

'No, no, I'm merely making observations.'

'Well. Have you been observing me?'

Stevens, confused, took out his cigarette case, and opened it.

'Here we are, two sheep in a storm,' said Lawless. 'We quarrel instead of trying to find a cave.'

Stevens did not offer Lawless a cigarette. Lawless watched nervously while the cigarette was being lit. Stevens was blowing out a cloud of smoke when Lawless said:

'Do you think tobacco soothes the nerves?'

'Would you like a cigarette?' said Stevens. 'Sorry, I understood you didn't smoke.'

'I feel ill,' said Lawless reaching out his gaunt hand.

Stevens tendered him the open cigarette case. The thin, long-nailed fingers fumbled about among the cigarettes before they could seize one. He put the cigarette between his lips, looked at Stevens furtively, and then threw the cigarette on the floor.

'Why not try one of my lozenges?' said Stevens. 'They are very good for the nerves.' He took out the packet and opened it.

Lawless furrowed his forehead and shook his head, 'Not drugs.'

'Not at all?'

'Well, they are supposed to have some curative quality.'

'I trust they have. In fact, I'm nearly sure, but my experiments are not yet......'

'You said God was a dream.'

'Did I? When?'

'Just now. That was my avenue of approach to God.'

'You won't have one of these lozenges?'

'No, no. Put them away. I want to talk to you. I tried to dream myself into that state and failed. Now, I'm like a... I feel like an empty tomb, out of which profane hands have stolen something holy. And my being vibrates with a sense of ghastly sacrilege.'

There was silence for a few moments.

'I think you're just starving yourself,' said Stevens. He sniffed the air. 'And the air here too. This is a very damp cottage. Not sufficient light either.' He coughed. 'Don't you notice any change in your condition since you came to live in this glen or have you always...' He stopped, suddenly noticing the strange way that Lawless was looking at him.

'Condition,' said Lawless rudely. 'My condition. Yes, of course, a sort of maniac or humbug, you are wondering which.'

'I'm sorry,' said Stevens.

But immediately Lawless lapsed into indifference again and turned back on his own thoughts. 'That old man visited me at night three days ago,' he said, 'or four. I forget which. He didn't come into the cottage. That's why I have not gone out since, hardly, except to milk the goats and to – but, since then I have felt a terrific depression, like...'

'Something he said, I suppose?'

'Yes and no. I have read too much. A man must scour his mind before he can absorb the truth. Because truth is an unknown essence and the wisdom of man is something artificial, merely an accumulation of words. Truth should come of its own accord, when the habitation is prepared.'

'Divine revelation.'

'Must you always mock?' said Lawless angrily.

'On the contrary. I never mock. You misunderstand me. But go on. Finish what you were saying. My own theories are more or less...'

'Never mind. I had tried to rush towards the end and he came just when I thought I had reached a stage where all human influence had vanished. My mind was like a crystal. I can still *see* what I felt then, but I no longer feel it, nor do I know how to get back to it.'

'Never mind,' said Stevens. 'You needn't trouble about that. Tomorrow or the next day you'll be in the same state.'

Lawless started. 'What do you mean?'

'He talked to you about ghosts?' asked Stevens.

'Yes.'

'And more or less threatened you?'

'More or less.'

'And asked you to listen to the birds flying.'

'Yes. '

'He did the same thing to me. I take it you couldn't... No. What happened when he went away?'

Lawless was trembling and did not reply. Stevens' brows had drawn together and his small eyes had a satiric expression.

'Why do you want to know that?'

'I assure you it's for no other purpose than to elucidate a certain theory. Might I hazard a guess? Will you honestly tell me if I'm wrong?'

'You see me,' said Lawless, with his trembling hands stretched out a little, 'you see me ill and you just...' He sneered with his lips. 'Yes. Go on. Two sick sheep and we bandy words. And all this while the storm grows. Go on, then, blabber.'

'You wanted to kill him.'

'You are the devil.'

'No, but you thought he was the devil.'

'Yes.' Lawless suddenly went lax and rested his chin on his hands. 'I could think of nothing else. All night I lay on my bed and whenever I closed my eyes I saw him fleeing and myself pursuing him with a knife. I have been three days in this house afraid to go out, for fear of meeting him, and this fear has utterly ruined me.'

'Macanasa is a very interesting character,' said Stevens coldly. 'But I didn't react in that way. Why? Simply because I'm neither God nor saint, and I never hope to be either. And for that reason it is not necessary for me to believe in devils or to believe any man is a devil.'

'Ha!' Lawless raised his head excitedly. 'One sheep has become a wolf. Beware.'

'Calm yourself.' Stevens' face was flushed. In spite of himself he had lost his temper. 'All you mystics believe that nobody has dreams but yourselves. Your attitude towards your less credulous fellow men is that of the soldier towards the civilian, contempt. The soldier's egoism is deliberately cultivated in order that he may throw away his life for nothing. But the mystic cultivates his egoism in order that he may become God. It's the old story of the frog, and when the frog is in danger of bursting he calls in science to comfort him. '

Lawless made a movement. Stevens held up his hand.

'You are ill,' he said, 'I can see you are ill. But you need your mind purged before you can begin to heal it. So listen. Humanity has produced thousands of saints, but it has been the explorers and thinkers who have made the Gods for the saints to worship. Every new tool and country and planet and natural force that is discovered by the patience and sacrifice of scientists and explorers and thinkers means a new aspect of God, a new God. Even now in Moscow they are marching round the tomb of Christ's successor. Let them march. You called me the devil just now because I am more interested in discovering things for myself than in marching round dead men's tombs, than in beating my breast and calling out for manna. But I, too, am looking for something. I came to this glen like you, looking for something. And possibly the cause of my coming was similar to yours. You were dissatisfied with life, and therefore you said it was ugly and wanted to set it in order at once.'

'That is untrue,' Lawless was getting very tired. 'I have no interest in life as you understand it.'

'How do you know how I understand life?' said Stevens aggressively.

'I also was disgusted with life. But more because of those who tried to reform it than because of the apathetic. At every step I found myself in the pursuit of knowledge, beset by howling fanatics, hypocrites, greedy louts and senseless revolutionaries. I found myself in a community that defies hatred and fear. In my position I had to be a hypocrite in order to avoid dismissal. And why? Because the institution where I lectured was controlled by priests who considered that a belief in a material hell was necessary for the salvation of mankind. I found myself forced to bow down before a false and hostile God in whose existence I did not believe. Until, by a lucky chance, I was enabled to come here, to freedom. Then you arrive to make another God, to fight me or those that will carry on my work when I'm dead.'

'Dead!' said Lawless dreamily, as if he were trying to remember something. He shook his head and said gently: 'Perhaps I have misjudged. Where there is fire there is truth. It is because I am unwell. You spoke of fear and hatred as the twin evils that corrupt the soul of man. It was what I also discovered. But why do you say that a God which would rid humanity of those evils would be hostile to you? Fear of death. Death. I had hopes of... As clear as I hear you speak now, but three short days ago, and now......'

'Of what had you hopes?' said Stevens sharply.

'Nothing,' said Lawless, looking into Stevens's eyes gently. 'Is not this the curse of man, that we two here, who have fled from fear and hatred, fear one another, and yet, unless we hurry to the light, death awaits us too. Already again I see a wall, an insurmountable wall, rising between my soul and yours, and yet we both are sheep, trembling before the coming storm and uttering loud brave words about trivial things... on either side of the wall we bleat.'

Stevens muttered something and rose from the window sill. He rubbed his chin with his left hand, looked at the floor shyly, and then leaned against the window sill once more. He crossed his feet and let his body go slack, with his chin resting against his chest. 'Had you reached the stage of believing yourself to be God?'

Lawless did not reply, but his eyes suddenly set. Gradually they began to gleam steadily.

'It is curious,' continued Stevens, 'that Nietzche, having joyfully announced that God was dead, later put on a white sheet and announced that he himself was God. Poetry is impossible unless there is a God. And God is good. There must be such, for it seems that life is an arch and God the centrepiece. But that God is the God we make and civilise, the mirror of our own perfection. Not the vision created by half savage minds, starved bodies and unsatisfied ambitions. He is an Imperial God, of Rome, Egypt, Persia, Greece, England, the apex of great civilisations, a forbearing God, with scales of justice and respect for knowledge. He is an accumulation of properties. But always, it seems, that somebody rises and overwhelms all that; just as the fanatic Christ roused the slaves against Rome.'

'You are a monster,' said Lawless.

'Yes,' Stevens was unmoved.

Lawless got to his feet unsteadily. His face became livid and it appeared that he was struggling with a desire to attack Stevens. He was like an aged lord struggling to rise and chastise with rods some impudent menial, grown bold.

'Yes,' said Stevens again. 'To rouse the slaves. See what you have done. Your efforts to reform the glen people. To banish fear and hatred. Today, very probably, blood will be spilt. It is always so.'

Lawless's hands clenched.

'Washed in the blood of the lamb,' continued Stevens coldly. 'The ancient Jews, overrun for centuries by the rival hordes of Egyptians and Babylonians, their women raped, their vineyards looted, their fig trees cut down, their men unsexed and beheaded, discovered a God of vengeance, washed in the blood of the Egyptians, Assyrians, Macedonians, and Romans. He smote them hip and thigh and did all manner of atrocities. Murder begets murder. The God of a people is always like the people. You can't get a hungry people to worship a genial

God. You can't get the people of this glen to stop being afraid until... well...' He rambled off into some incoherent mutterings and put his hand in his pocket where he crackled the paper that contained the lozenges. 'Yes, the Irish. The land of sorrows. Washed in the blood of the English. A God in the new style, may I ask? To plunge the world into a new crusade. Hardly that. Their word is their bond. Just like the Romans. Gravitas, etc. Newton, Darwin, Stevenson. All sober men. And then the remains of beautiful cities you see on the African coast, with foul Arabs tending their stinking goats among the ruins of Roman grandeur. So will England be washed in the blood of some new stinking religion. And man will be again robbed for centuries of the fruits of science and civilisation. By fanatics who are bursting with egomania and wish to do themselves what requires millions of brains, working in unison...' Suddenly he pulled out the packet of lozenges. 'This may be my contribution,' he cried. 'May do more to achieve immortality than all the ravings of the prophets.'

'You monster,' shouted Lawless, darting forward.

Stevens moved to the left sharply. Lawless reached the window. Then he gasped with pain. His eyes had become bloodshot, and as he looked at Stevens, their expression changed rapidly from anger to sadness. Although he was silent, it seemed that an agonising appeal issued from his eyes, as they sank down into some fathomless abyss.

Then he staggered and muttered: 'Give me your hand.. please.'

'Poor devil,' said Stevens tenderly, gripping him about the body.

CHAPTER X

Lawless had fainted. When he opened his eyes again it was almost dark. He was in bed. Instead of the rough army blanket, he found over him two warm blankets and a quilt. And there were fresh white sheets on the bed. He was not surprised at this, immediately after awakening. Instead he felt very comfortable. The window was wide open and clean. He himself had never opened it nor cleaned the panes. And through the window he could see tree branches, dusk-enshrouded, waving languorously in the night breeze. Birds twittered. And through the tree branches the rising land passed upwards dimly, like a sheltering wall, to an unseen horizon. He was encompassed snugly, by the earth, by the night and by the warmth that friendly hands had laid about his body.

He did not trouble to inquire how this had come to pass. As he lay awake, it seemed to him that he was very happy. A strange memory entered his mind of the village which his father had owned. There, in the evening, driving slowly through the village street with his mother and sisters, he often saw bright fires burning on hearths, with village women rocking their babies to sleep and crooning songs to them. That was very beautiful. But then it had appeared remote and foreign and hostile. His mother's face had always borne a proud and contemptuous look, and he himself had been conscious only of the bare feet, blue with cold and the servile look on the dirty faces of the people. But now the people were near, friendly and beautiful. Everything was at peace and the sea that rolled embroidered with foam to the black headland beyond his father's demesne was beautiful too and friendly, even though he used to fear it and thought it was the ghostly voice of the evicted peasant Bartly Hynes, who had died in the workhouse cursing 'every man that ever bears the name of Lawless.'

Through the open door of the bedroom he heard women's voices in the sitting room. He listened to them eagerly, first without paying any heed to the words, but joyfully listening to the sounds. Hearing them he knew that he had considered himself all his life an outcast from the people and that their blind hatred of his caste had driven him on, on, seeking to find a way, through some subterfuge, into their confidence. But had they hated him? Those urchins with cold, bare feet and dirty faces, smirking subserviently with their obstinate lips? Listening to the subdued voices of the women, his vanity rose up before his mind, enormous like a mountain that bursts with the heat of a volcano and belches forth its bowels in lava. He shed soft tears and murmured inwardly. 'I see why I have done all this. Afraid of their hatred. The wise teacher sits in the valley among the people, for in the high places the wind distorts their voices into strange forms.'

'An' dy'e ever think, Mrs. Deegan,' whispered Mrs. Dillon in the sitting room, 'of all the years we spend down here in this hole, without ever having a bit of fun, an' all that time the grave is waiting for us and we are moving towards it down into the earth? We get up and we work and we eat a bite and we curse at one another and we grudge one another the ground we walk on, and we never think of the time we'll all be dead. God! How I hate this hole! Sometimes I listen and can't hear a thing but them bloody mountains standing grey all round me like prison walls. Why don't the people rise up and –'

'God sent us here,' said the gruff voice of Mrs. Deegan. 'Maybe those that'll come after us'll have an easier life. But we do what we can do and the Infant Saviour'll reward us. In the schools now they are teaching them fine things.'

'And what odds will that make?' cried Mrs. Dillon eagerly. 'Look at Mr. Lawless that was reared like a lord with lashins wherever he turned his head all round him. And him lying there on that bed all the afternoon and evening seeing devils and Dr. Stevens giving him medicine to calm him down.'

Lawless trembled and then lay very still listening.

'I never think at all,' muttered Mrs. Deegan. 'God between us and harm. God makes us so tired with work, and its a blessing. We just lie down and sleep. For when we have small mouths to feed and cattle to look after and the rent to pay what time is there? In the old days I heard them say, when the people worked for taskmasters and no wages, they used to stand in the fields and say: "God curse you sun, you are a long time going west and we from the dawn of day fasting." My grandfather used to tell me that. Times are better now and we should be thankful to God's Blessed Mother.'

Lawless shuddered. There was silence in the kitchen. Then he heard Mrs. Dillon's voice, fierce but almost inaudible.

'If I were working for a taskmaster without pay I'd murder him.'

'You say that,' muttered Mrs. Deegan. 'It's easy talking. But my father often told me that an empty stomach has no hands. It's hard for a fallen ass to rise under a load. The load must be taken off him first. Now people have the land.'

'And much good it does them, Mrs. Deegan. I'm only a young woman yet, but I remember when I was a little girl that we were better off and everybody too, when the gentry were in the country. I was born in the Big House, ye know. Me mother was working in it and me father too. There was always a clean place and nice food and it did ye good to see the gentry passing to and fro, carriages and horses and dogs, women with gold ornaments on them that thick, and officers from England with uniforms that ud make yer mouth water. There was a snatch for everybody, tips and dances and drinks flying around.'

'God curse them,' said Mrs. Deegan bitterly, 'they bled us and ground us down. The bread of charity is bitter. My father often said a dog's life is hunger and ease, kicks six days and a full belly on a Sunday. We have the land. By our own power we took it and salt on your own hearth is better than butter in the master's kitchen. And we'll keep it, too. There is work now for our hands and maybe little Johnny'll grow up into another world altogether. They say there'll be big things done soon and jobs going in the city.'

'What good is it?' murmured Mrs. Dillon dreamily. 'It's a come down for me, that's all I know. And I don't care, Mrs. Deegan, what happens to me children or to meself either, for me heart is sore in me, so I could grind the stones with me teeth when I think of how I'm placed here with the world jigging beyond the mountains.'

'Don't tell yer sorrows to the neighbours nor to the mountains either, for God listens. We were put into this world to save our immortal souls and to do our work proper, as God thought fit to give us, and rear our children. And when we're gone they'll gather what we sow. And it's the best thing that will be remembered of us that we did our work proper, praising God.'

'Ye needn't tell me that, Mrs. Deegan,' said Mrs. Dillon excitedly. 'I've had cross words with ye and we didn't speak to each other now for a month, but you're a good neighbour, what I can't say for many. But ye know as well as me that them that hasn't the fear o' God in their hearts prosper better than the good. Look at them Macanasas, highway robbers and schemers that's gone and turned the glen into a bedlam with their dogs. Aren't they prospering? They are grabbing everything with their dirty hands. Four sons and they all too mean to marry. And a daughter so proud she won't speak to the people. Said her people owned this glen once. Like hell they did. They grudged us the bit of grass our cattle ate on Lawless's land. As if it belonged to them. It's all right for you. You have a good man and three sons and – and ye never knew different.'

'They'll not hear the last of them dogs for a long time,' said Mrs. Deegan dourly. 'If it costs me the last penny I have, I'll have revenge. Aye, if I have to open his rotten skull with a hatchet and hang for it, so help me God.'

'It's no good, Mrs. Deegan,' said Mrs. Dillon. 'There is no use struggling. Everybody is against the poor. Look at Mr. Lawless,' she added in a whisper, 'that never touched a hair of any man's head. They're all against him. Him that was a landlord's son an' he trying to help the people. They say he was put in jail for it, and now he's lying there without a soul to care for him, as if he were a pauper. Oh! Mrs. Deegan, we often think bad of others without cause. There's Dr. Stevens, with little eyes like a Chinaman, and he's gone to all this trouble for Mr. Lawless. He must have a heart of gold after all.'

'My father often said,' murmured Mrs. Deegan, 'that sickness binds the people together. Sure even the pagans help the sick.'

'God! Mrs. Deegan,' whispered Mrs. Dillon, 'I've been tidying up here all the afternoon and ye know I'd be happy if I could work and tend for a man like that. Ye should see the things that are in that room. Like a monk he must be. There's a skull on the table. Did ye see it?'

'Hush, don't talk of it,' said Mrs. Deegan nervously. 'Poor man, maybe he means no harm and a sick man is under God's protection, whoever he be. But after that sermon today I feel it isn't altogether right to – but sure a sick man even if he were a cannibal is –'

'Much I care for their sermons,' retorted Mrs. Dillon. 'Let them preach. It's not their bellies are empty. It's too much we're listening to their bloody sermons.'

'Woman! '

'That's all right. The ground won't open. I'm tellin' you, Mrs. Deegan, that the day'll come when something'll happen to them fellahs, terrifying the people about hell, and then stealing the people's money.'

'Hush, will ye. God forgive ye.'

'I will not. Why can't everybody get an opportunity same as – God! I wish I were a man. When I came back from Mass and saw Larry running after the cattle and your man shouting and swearing, I just felt that I could take a gun and shoot – shoot –'

'Who?'

'Everybody,' she muttered. 'Why don't the people rise up and shoot. But they never shoot the right people. Same as when the civil war was on. It was always the wrong people that were shot. Everything is always wrong and the poor people are always left in holes like this, with the master's heel on their neck.'

'Oh! It's no use talking like that,' said Mrs. Deegan. 'It's better to obey the law of God and man. Hush, who's this?'

'Its an indictment,' murmured Lawless, 'an indictment.' Perspiration was pouring from him.

'Well!' he heard Dr. Stevens's voice say. 'How is he?'

'He's asleep yet.'

'Hm! Here I brought a little drop of brandy. I thought you might like a drop.'

'Oh! God bless ye, sir,' said Mrs. Deegan, 'sure we wouldn't know ourselves.'

'I never take anything stronger than port, sir,' said Mrs. Dillon.

'Never mind. I wonder are there any glasses? I'll have a look.'

Dr. Stevens entered the bedroom on his way to the kitchen, saw Lawless awake and paused. 'Hello. How do you feel now?'

Lawless thrust out his hand from under the bedclothes. Stevens advanced. As they shook hands Lawless said: 'Thanks. Thanks. I've put you to a deal of trouble.'

'Oh! That's... I fancy it was a little... a little overwrought, I fancy. I haven't the necessary.... here, you see... medical etiquette, but from the examination I made, there's nothing. I put it down to... well, let us say, nervous prostration resulting from.... you should clear out of this place.'

Lawless released Stevens's hand. 'I heard these women talking. Who are they?'

'Just a moment,' said Stevens. 'Have you any glasses in the house?'

'No, but you'll find some cups in the kitchen. I kept some thinking perhaps that some poor man might come in and...'

'Right. May I look?'

Stevens went into the kitchen, found the cups on a table covered with dust, cleaned them and brought them into the room where the women were. He gave each some brandy. Each blessed him and his ancestors. Then he returned to Lawless's room and closed the door behind him. It was very dark in the room.

'Have you no light?'

'No,' said Lawless. 'I don't keep any light in the house... except a little lamp in the far room... in my study. If you wish, you may...'

'This is very well as it is. I have put a fire in your sitting room.' Stevens sat on the side of the bed. He took Lawless's hand and felt the pulse. 'Sounds all right now. How do you feel? Weak, I suppose?'

'Weak! Not at all.' He tried to rise and could not.

'Just lie still and don't worry. You must have become over excited. A little rest, that's all.'

'I heard two women talking. One with an eager, young voice. Who is she?'

'That's Mrs. Dillon.'

'I was listening to them. What a life! We never experience that.'

'What were they discussing?'

'The misery of their existence. You know it was that which first made me want to do something. But it seems that everything I did went wrong because I never understood. Everybody should be born poor. It is only the poor who have wisdom.'

'I am of the people.'

'Ah!'

'For that reason I have no pity for them.'

'I am beginning to understand you. If you have no pity why have you done all this for me?'

'Don't disturb yourself. We'll discuss that tomorrow. You need food now. Some milk and an egg. I got Mrs. Dillon to milk your goats. Couldn't manage it myself. I'm afraid I'm still a town dweller, though my father's people scratched about on land as barren and wild as this. Seems so crude, harnessing an animal's sex instincts to provide food. Much simpler when we can manufacture it. Do you feel hungry?'

'I want to talk to you about things... I'm in an awful mess.'

'Not now. Tomorrow. Don't trouble yourself.' Stevens got to his feet.

Lawless grasped his hand and kissed it. Stevens walked away embarrassed. He went into the sitting room. Both women, having finished their brandy, were whispering together in a happy way and the glad smiles on their faces betokened an affection for one another, for the world and their own condition in it, altogether unexpected from their recent conversation.

'How is he, sir?' asked Mrs. Dillon.

'I think you might go home now, Mrs. Deegan,' said Stevens. 'They'll probably want you. Thanks very much for your help. Perhaps you might bring a few eggs in the morning and a little fresh buttermilk if you have any.'

'Yes, sir. In the morning. Yes sir. Good night now, sir, and may God look down on us all. We know neither the day nor the hour, but His help is nearer nor the door.'

'Amen,' said Mrs. Dillon in a whisper.

'Good night,' said Stevens, as Mrs. Deegan went out. 'You'll find your way all right?'

'Yes, sir,' she answered from the gate.

'I wonder could you cook an egg?' he said to Mrs. Dillon. 'Before you go, unless you are in a hurry.'

She immediately sprang to work with fierce energy. And it was good to see her, who was so slovenly in her own house, work here with such neatness and speed. Lawless, lying on the bed, listened to all her movements, and when she passed through the bedroom on her way to the kitchen and back, his eyes devoured her. She was so young, so lithe, so active. And when she glanced shyly at him passing, her brilliant eyes were as wild as those of a young filly which peasants have brought down to a sandy shore to tame. Held with long manilla ropes on either side, she prances, snorting, while the sunlight fills her black eyes with shining spears. Her rude, disordered hair, black like still water on a moonless night, hung about her slender head in turbulent confusion, a glorious crown on such a rebellious, passionate body.

With delicate hands she offered him food shyly, breathing hard, with downcast eyes, in silence. And then she left without a word. She ran out and in the yard he heard her mutter a curse at something. When Stevens called to her from the sitting room she yelled something from afar in reply.

Stevens came into the bedroom with something in a glass.

'Drink this first,' he said, stirring with a spoon. 'It's a little medicine. Best I can do. Won't do any harm, anyway. It's just a good guess. But I'm practically certain.'

Lawless had been eagerly listening to the departing sounds of feet. He started up and looked at Stevens. Then he looked at the medicine. His face became cautious.

'Still experimenting?'

'Very well, don't take it.'

'Give it me,' said Lawless, and he tossed it off.

'Now eat.'

'I do feel hungry,' said Lawless, turning to the food.

'Ha! Good,' Stevens rubbed his hands together. 'I thought so. Splendid.' He took up the empty glass that had contained the medicine, and although it was empty, he began to stir it with the spoon. He smiled at the wall in a childish way. Then he sat down and watched Lawless eat. Lawless ate ravenously, in silence. Now and again he paused and glanced out of the window listening. Then he would glance at Stevens and flush. He finished his food.

'Now try to sleep,' said Stevens. 'We'll have that conversation tomorrow.'

'What conversation?' Lawless seemed to have forgotten. Altogether there was a marked change in his face. His eyes roved about restlessly. His thin, pale face, disfigured by a thick growth of hair, was very queer. And the way he began to touch his lips together slightly when he looked out the window!

'What the devil is he up to now?' thought Stevens. 'I had better spend the night here.'

CHAPTER XI

Later, there was a moon that lit the room with a ghostly light. Lawless slept on his back, and many times during the night he stirred restlessly, thinking someone was bending over him, examining his features. Then he shut his eyes tightly and feverish dreams disturbed his mind.

He dreamed all night, one long recurring dream of a wild-haired woman. A horse-tamer, leading many men among mountains. She rode a black stallion and galloped along a frozen river, with her hair flying loose among the horse's mane. Naked she was and he pursued her closely. Often she looked behind and beckoned to him with open arms, gripping her hair between her laughing teeth. But every time he plunged forward to mount the stallion with her, the ice broke and he sank down, through jingling ice, a jingle for every sin, floating, whirling icicles, whirling downwards.

Lo! She re-appeared and there was no more sin, nor warmth of blood, nor fire of human passion, but the virgin purity of clouds. For she floated among cloud mists, and armed with a great bird's wings he hovered over her with flapping wings. Nothing was visible of her but her hair and her flashing teeth. For her limbs were clouds and his wings touched and touched the misty edges of her being trying to call her. Higher up she went, until the firmament was full of floating birds, each bird a winged soul pursuing and sheltering a misty phantom.

And everything was flooded with a golden light and a fairy sound of music issued softly about the floating winged mists and flashing teeth. Until a little bird, with little eyes, came rushing with wild screams among the floating souls, tearing the mists with his sharp beak and all fell down in showering bitter hail, for many years, for endless aeons of years, fell without stopping through the bitter hail and went on falling, oh, so bitterly.

CHAPTER XII

Wrapped in a heavy overcoat, Stevens watched by Lawless's bedside. He had tried to find in the house some material for a bed, but he could find nothing excepting old clothes in the kitchen. So he put the stool against the wall and sat on it. He lit a cigarette and began to think, with his chin resting on his hand. Now and again he rose to watch the sleeper's face. Then he would sit again and think and listen to the night sounds of the valley and to the motion of the heavy air.

'What a strange being!' he thought. 'The fascination caused by wilful self-destruction hypnotises the reason. Is that not so? Did Nero burn Rome? When the pine trees on that hill caught fire, I myself watched it with delight and I hated the men that rushed to quench it. How beautifully cruel were the flames, leaping from tree to tree, flashing from clouds of smoke, like Jove's thunderbolts. Why, I wonder? And the silly black figures of the shouting men rushing hither and thither... There he is now. Of course a fool, and yet I feel something mightily powerful in this queer room, other than myself. He believes so much. If one could only believe like that, perhaps, after all, one might burn beautifully. But how silly it all is! How infinitely silly! '

He began to smile and thought of a cattle drover he had met the week before, while tramping to a distant lake among the mountains. A funny, lewd, drunkard of a man, beating a shackled bull with a heavy stick, as he drove him over the mountain road. He talked of women and drinking bouts, of jails where he had lain. The man said he had only one rib unbroken. He ate cow's udder. A raw brute. But amusing. He had no ruminative mind that squealed with fear when there were noises at night in the mountains. No God. An animal. What did he care? And is there greater joy than flesh lusts and taut sinews struggling in battle?

He shuddered and stamped out his cigarette. 'Morbid!' he thought. 'Everything must turn morbid near this sleeper. Now he is just like any other man asleep. See him tossing in his dreams. What of? Some fool's paradise. I bet the drover never dreamt. Unless he ravished some woman in his sleep. And I? What am I doing here? I think perhaps after all it is better to run with the herd and scream at night when there are shadows on the mountains. To make Gods and worship them. And perhaps I, too, shall make a little God and go through the world showing my new toy to all humanity. Eureka! A fire of wood. An iron plough. A gun. A drug to kill the consciousness of pain. Christ! What's that?'

It was only the moon, lighting the room, with her yellow light. It drifted slowly inwards, the corpse-light of a dead world, the wandering spirit of the burnt moon. It made no sound. There was no glitter in its rays, no spears of fire, givers of warmth. It was nothing but a weird phantom, flitting silently. What hailed it? Carolling birds, or stretching, yawning beasts or wild barbarian men awakening in forests? Nothing. No sound. All slept.

Stevens stood up, walked on tiptoe to the window and looked out. He saw the moon, the mountains and the trees. He heard a frog croaking. He saw, in the moonlight, a huddled rabbit feeding on a grassy mound. The air was sweet. And seeing all this, all became real again and as it should be, an ordered comeliness of sweet air, silent spaces and gentle, gentle light. What could a puny man do to disturb such majesty?

Fortified, he returned to the bedside and looked closely at the sleeper. The slight body lay still on its right side, facing him. The left knee was bent, overlapping the right thigh. The left hand lay stretched down over the quilt, the long limp fingers curved and twitching gently. The right hand was stretched out flat on the bed beneath, bare to the elbow, so white and delicate, a beautiful thing, a thing to gesture with, like a wand. The haggard, bearded face was now reflecting the distant, exalted imaginings of the mind. The brilliant eyes were closed but the parted lips seemed to speak of and see and feel an immeasurable beauty. They moved constantly.

Stevens sat again on his stool. He lit another cigarette. When he struck the match the sleeper moved and murmured something. Stevens closed his eyes and dozed a little. His cigarette went out. Then he started suddenly and sat up. He listened. It was only the goats marching on the roof of the shed. Something had disturbed them. One bleated a low cry, short, querulous, a question. Nothing answered. A snort. Then silence again. Looking at the moon, on the rooftop, side by side? Why?

Stevens relit his cigarette. He thought of the glory of man, the fearless pursuit in which he himself took part, seeking for knowledge. There was no horizon to this territory. No jumbled words passed as fetishes to affect a lordship over the searching minds. Searchers who had discovered a universe a million times as large as the one created by Jehovah, God of the Jews. Sun upon sun and constellations reaching to infinity. Today they had roamed the earth, fallen over its edge and found that it was round. Tomorrow they would invade the firmament in ships bound for the new El Dorado.

'My dust,' he thought arrogantly, 'if not myself. What am I doing here, watching this illiterate barbarian! He abolish death! Already he is half a corpse – a starved weakling. See his twitching hands. All the sneers of society have begotten this disease in him. Curse you, you boor, I was happy before you came. Now there is some damn disease in this valley. It's foul. I feel it.'

He got to his feet again and put his hands in his pockets. Then he smiled and sat down again. He rubbed his face with his palms, glanced at Lawless, and smiled again. 'It's no use,' he thought. 'There he is. I know very well... yet. Poor fellow! Why poor? He's richer than I? He overawes me. I'm afraid of him. What a terrible feeling! What must it have been when Christ was crucified?'

A curious feeling now took possession of him. He wanted to laugh aloud, to poke Lawless in the ribs, to pull the bedclothes off him, to spit on him, to whisper foul things in his ear. That terrified him and he got to his feet. He listened and raised his eyebrows and opened his mouth wide. Then the feeling returned with greater force; but at the same time he had a vision of his childhood, of his home and of his father half asleep after a hard day's work in the fields, reciting the evening prayers, while all the family knelt around the hearth sleepily, 'Lighten our darkness we beseech Thee O Lord,' while he himself knelt crouching over a chair dreaming of the future and calculating problems with the stump of a pencil. He closed his mouth and gasped.

A violent fit of merriment followed. He bent over the bed and whispered, quite inaudibly: 'Say, Lawless. Get up and give a sign. Raise the dead. Be a sport. Do you hear? Cure yourself first, though.'

Still smiling, he sat down and began to eat lozenges. Then he fell asleep.

CHAPTER XIII

When Stevens awoke he immediately looked at the bed. Lawless was not there. He jumped up and ran to the window. The morning was already far advanced. The dew had dried on the grass. All was still. Stevens pulled off his heavy overcoat and walked to the door. Then he paused, came back to the bed and examined it. Lawless had taken off his pyjamas and put on his other clothes, and there was a wet towel hanging on the rail of the bed.

'That's all right,' said Stevens. 'He must be all right again.' He looked at his watch. It was eight o'clock. He decided to go home and have breakfast. In the sitting room he found a can of milk on the window sill. Lawless had milked the goats. The door was wide open. He went out into the yard and glanced around casually, expecting to see Lawless there. There was nobody there and the goats had also left. Although there was nothing extraordinary in this, Stevens had a feeling that something was wrong.

'Oh! I'll just go home to breakfast.' He said. 'The fellow is quite mad. Why should I bother with him?'

He went into the house, got his overcoat, and came out once more into the yard. There he paused and scratched his head. 'What'll you bet,' he said to himself, 'that he hasn't gone for good? These fellows are here one day and in China the next. Can't get on without women. Oh! By Jove! '

He struck his forehead and hurried out to the gate. There was nobody in sight except Deegan's little son, a long way up the mountainside to the right, driving three slow cows to the pasture. Stevens went to the left along the path leading to Dillon's house. He climbed to the top of the wooden gate leading into Dillon's land and looked about him. At first he could see nobody, but presently he saw two figures standing within a copse some distance to the left of the house, where there was a sort of ford crossing a stream.

'There he is,' said Stevens to himself. 'I was right.'

He climbed down from the gate on the far side and walked off to the left through Dillon's fields, going towards his own house across the river. The two figures were almost directly in the path. And he had not gone far when they suddenly emerged from the copse. It was not Mrs. Dillon, but her husband, Larry Dillon. Lawless was gesticulating and talking eagerly. The two goats also came out of the copse behind Lawless. Dillon was carrying a dead rabbit. Stevens walked on until he was close to them without their noticing him. He was just going to call out to Lawless when he heard Lawless's voice, talking to Dillon, say distinctly:

'I am very glad you agree to this. I'll get the matter arranged properly in legal fashion. Just consult your wife, and if she agrees, you come up to the cottage later. I'll wait for you there. I think the matter...'

The two of them passed Stevens, quite close, apparently without seeing him. Stevens looked after them, two men, one tall, slim, moving gracefully, a proud and kingly figure, the other small, uncouth, with slithering gait, a base body carrying dead prey. They parted. Lawless walked on, upright, without pausing, towards his house. Dillon walked slowly homewards with downcast head. Stevens watched. A collie bitch came bounding towards Dillon, circled around him sniffing the air and then with outstretched snout she darted at the dead rabbit. Dillon halted, swung the dead rabbit above the collie's head and laughed. The collie put her fore feet on Dillon's hip and gazed at the rabbit, her lolling red tongue hung out and shining in the sunlight. She yapped. Dillon walked on again, kicking the grass, while the collie pawed and licked the dangling dead rabbit.

Lawless climbed over the fence into his own land. The goats followed him to the top of the fence and remained there, standing. Lawless's head bobbed up and down, passing away. It disappeared.

Stevens hated him, and as he walked hurriedly it seemed that a ferocious trait in his character had suddenly found cause to come to life. Between his throat and his chest something irritated a passionate desire. And he walked bending forward, closing his eyes and opening them, like a person in pain. He became enraged with life and he wanted to assault things, stab animals, embrace trees, shout. Yet all this was impossible. And he walked on, stooping. It was pleasant to hate. Crossing the bridge he met Macanasa. The fellow was sitting there at the far end with his chin stuck in the air, scratching the stubble on his hairy neck.

'He's after her,' thought Stevens. 'That woman is a...'

'Good morning, Dr. Stevens,' said Macanasa, getting to his feet. 'Yer out early. And sure, Glory be to God, it's a fine morning and why wouldn't ye be out watching the colours that does be on the mountains with the rising sun? They say Mr. Lawless is sick.'

'I'm afraid you're going to get into trouble,' said Stevens.

'God between us and harm,' said Macanasa, 'and why is that?'

The two men were side by side, Macanasa peering closely into Stevens' face.

'It's up all night ye were watching the mountains,' he said. 'They say there are mines there hidden. Gold and silver, the old people said, and the fairies do be all night counting it. It's many a thing a man like yer honour 'ud be doing at night when poor people are asleep. And what d'ye say now I'd get into trouble?'

'What about your dogs?' said Stevens.

'Oh! Me curse on them,' said Macanasa. 'They're gone. They went mad, and we had to drown them in the lake last night. Two fine dogs. 'Twill be hard to find their like. Me son is gone to the town today to buy a pair. They went mad and chased the neighbours' cattle, an' I asleep. And sure I wouldn't get into trouble over that.'

'Oh! I don't know.'

'And is it Mr. Lawless 'ud take the law of me now? They say he is a holy man. They tell me he was sick, but I saw him talking in the field to Larry Dillon a minute ago.'

'Yes, he's well again.'

'A holy man, but queer in the head. Now what would he be talking to Larry Dillon for? Maybe it would be best to talk to him and beg his honour's pardon. About the dogs. Me curse on them dogs. I took me cattle across the river for fear the Deegans 'ud maim them in the night. Oh! There's a curse on that land. Maybe it's how he's bringing the Dillons to live with him. She's a great woman surely, that wife of Larry Dillon's. A great worker and a darling woman. She lived in the city and she has comely ways and a comely face too. But sure, yer honour, that kissed the hands of great ladies, wouldn't pay heed to her, beggin' yer honour's pardon.'

'Yes, perhaps you had better talk to him,' said Stevens, flushing. 'I must go home to breakfast.'

'And why wouldn't ye?' said Macanasa. 'God bless ye.'

'Does he know something?' thought Stevens, walking up the slope. 'How did I get into the hands of that slut? I'm beginning to get afraid of the people. There's something weird about them. But won't that help my...

But what if I myself were becoming a victim? I've been here a year.'

Going towards Lawless's house Macanasa met Mrs. Deegan. She was bringing the eggs and buttermilk which Dr. Stevens had asked her to bring. When she saw Macanasa she began to shout: 'May your road be crooked and thorny wherever you are going,' she cried. 'And may you never come back. May the shriek of dawn be heard in your house before the sun rises again. And may the devil scald your carcase after a terrible death, without priest or Extreme Unction. A hag's curse on you, you servant of the devil. Your eyes turn the food sour in the stomachs of your neighbours' children.'

Macanasa leaned on his stick and made answer. 'It's a sour hag's voice you have,' he said. 'And the child growing in your womb will have my curse on it for the devil's words that came out of your mouth, you ragged whore. Turn back now with your bribes in your hands and sit on the dunghill with a sack over your head and scratch your face with thorns, for it was by the devil's order you came. No man nor woman will drink milk off this land while the blood is warm in a Macanasa.'

'Bribery is it?' she cried, dashing the eggs she carried against a stone.

'What I take I take by law and no bribery, but I'll call the Holy Mother of God to be my witness that you'll rot in jail or I'll die a murderer.'

'Murder is it, woman?' he cried. 'Your husband's blood'll be dripping off my hands if ye don't run for yer life.' 'Murderer,' he cried. 'Murderer.'

She turned and ran back to the house. The can of milk jerked against her running body and the milk squirted out. She shouted as she ran. 'We'll take ye to the county town before the month is out and we'll perjure our immortal souls to lay ye low, ye murderer.'

'Go now,' he said, shaking his stick and spitting. 'Go now, you hag.'

He followed her to the gate that led into her land and he closed the gate tightly after her. Then he put a few pieces of gorse on the top of it, crying out: 'Be gone now, you hag. Be gone now.'

Then he hurried off towards Lawless's house. 'They won't put another foot on this land,' he muttered.

When he came to the gate Lawless was walking up and down the yard with his hands behind his back. He did not hear Macanasa coming because he was excitedly watching Dillon's house, waiting for an answer to his proposal. Macanasa hailed him from the gate. Lawless started violently and turned about.

'What?' he shouted in a terrified voice. 'You here again?'

'It's about the allegations they are making, yer honour,' said Macanasa.

'Be gone, be gone,' cried Lawless, putting his hands to his eyes. 'Why do you persecute me?'

Macanasa peered through the bars of the gate. 'Could I come in to light me pipe, yer honour?' he said. 'I want to put meself right with ye about them dogs.'

'Stay outside,' cried Lawless, warning him with his hand.

'Now, Mr. Lawless, don't believe evil of me. Them dogs was mad, and that's how it was. They went mad, and they're drowned already.'

Lawless began to pace back and forth, gripping his hands behind his back.

'It's me is yer friend and not them people,' said Macanasa. 'But the good man is always left standing at the gate while the wicked are souping in the house. But I'll raise my voice, so I will, to the high King of Heaven, and may the sky fall on my mangled body if I utter a word of a lie. For it is mad they went, and I asleep by the river. And is it the first time dogs went mad, when everybody remembers in this glen the bulldog that Colonel Chaundy had? He bit the right thumb off a cattle drover from Moyness and the lad was brought to the doctor in town. The surgeons killed the dog, so they did. They locked him in a box and poured chloroform into it out of a big bag, so the postman said. And me drover lad roamed the roads for years after with the stump of a thumb that the children used to make fun of. Until one day he went for a drink of milk into a house at Ballycarron and the woman said to him and he going to drink the milk: "Was that dog mad," says she, "that took a bite out of you?" He threw the milk in her face. He let a screech out of him and ran out of the house, and he's mad from that day to this, locked up in a padded cell in the asylum. For he saw the dog in the milk when the words came out of her mouth. But, yer honour, the dogs didn't come near ye, did they?'

Lawless looked at him in fear.

'They say dogs are queer,' continued the old man, 'when they are mad. And if ye see one in a dream it's a sign.'

'Be gone,' cried Lawless again. 'Go away. Go away!'

'I'm going,' said the old man. 'But if ye didn't follow them with stones, as it was told to me ye did, no harm will come to ye.'

'What are you talking about?' said Lawless, coming to the gate.

'Didn't I tell ye the place was haunted?' said Macanasa, moving away. 'There are many roads leading down into this house, but there's only one leading out of it, once the good people cast their eye on the dweller.'

'Be gone, ruffian.'

'That's the road to the grave. But sure yer honour has no fear of death they say.'

Suddenly they heard people approach. Dillon, his wife and his two children were coming through the boundary gate.

'Ho, then,' cried Macanasa, becoming excited. 'This place is full of grabbers. Who's coming now?'

'Friend, friend,' cried Lawless, waving to Dillon, 'come quickly. Turn this man off.'

'Turn me off is it,' said Macanasa, 'off me people's land. Is it you 'ud turn me off, Larry Dillon?'

Dillon did not reply, but Mrs. Dillon approached rapidly, pushing an extraordinary little perambulator in which her young child was strapped.

'Faith, ye better be gone before I lay hands on ye,' she said to Macanasa.

'I'm going,' said Macanasa, 'but the priest'll lay his hands on you.'

'Aye, and the police'll lay their hands on you,' said Mrs. Dillon, 'when we are done with ye. Bring all yer sons and yer lump of a wife too and yer skinny daughter. We're not afraid of them. Fitter for ye to put yer idiot of an epileptic son in a home nor to be aggravating yer neighbours and maiming their cattle.'

'Don't mind him, sir,' she said to Lawless.

'Be God he will mind me,' shouted Macanasa from a distance as he hurried off. 'And you will too. Ye're entering the house gay enough, but ye won't come out of it so gay. I'll give ye my word for that.'

He halted and waved back his stick. 'Turn back before ye pass the gate,' he called.

Mrs. Dillon stuck out her tongue at him. Then she wheeled her perambulator in through the gate Lawless had opened for her, dragging the other child after her. Her husband also slouched in. Lawless closed the gate. Then he hurried on in front towards the door, continually turning around, smiling and beckoning to them, his face exalted, his eyes gleaming, his body trembling. And they followed him slowly, the woman's eyes wild, the man's eyes shrewd and suspicious. They all entered the house.

CHAPTER XIV

The priest did not reach the glen that day. He had been detained in another part of the parish owing to the sudden illness of a wealthy old lady. The people, however, did not take any notice of his absence, because the arrival of the priest, usually such an important event, was robbed of its importance by the rapidly increasing tension that gathered around Lawless's cottage. Tragedy always approaches with a comic aspect. It is only when the watchers detect something mystical in the burlesque demeanour and acoutrements of the approaching buffoon that the tragedy becomes apparent. The extraordinary event with which this narrative terminates had, in a similar manner, on this day begun to herald its approach.

Determined to have revenge on Macanasa and still covetous of Lawless's land, Mrs. Deegan incited her husband to go to the village for the purpose of getting a summons issued against Macanasa. Deegan, therefore, timorous of going alone, went to see Dillon, hoping to get him to go also. On his way to Dillon's house he met Dillon and his family coming out of Lawless's cottage. Lawless was standing in his doorway, smiling, with his hands folded on his chest, gazing at the ground in front of him. Deegan tipped his cap in Lawless's direction and then stepped aside under the fence. He beckoned to Dillon.

'I'm going to the village about that,' he said. 'Are ye comin'?'

'Come on Larry,' said Mrs. Dillon, dragging her child and her perambulator after her. 'Ye have no time to waste bladdering with people.'

She went off without saying a word to Deegan. Dillon was following his wife, also without speaking, when Deegan stepped forward and caught him by the shoulder.

'What's this about, Larry?' he said.

Dillon looked at him arrogantly. Deegan was amazed at the extraordinary transformation that had taken place in the man's countenance. It looked vicious instead of weak, arrogant instead of being servile, impertinent, although it had hitherto been meek.

'Who are ye layin' hold of?' said Dillon.

'Have ye forgotten that summons?' said Deegan. 'Are ye funkin' it? Is it afraid of Macanasa ye are?'

'Come on Larry,' cried Mrs. Dillon.

'Lemme go,' said Dillon, pushing off Deegan's hand. 'I'm afraid o' nobody. I've business o' me own, though, to do in the village today.'

'Shut yer bloody mouth,' called Mrs. Dillon, 'and come on.'

'Aren't ye goin' to draw the summons with me?' yelled Deegan.

'I'm not drawing any summons,' muttered Dillon, moving away. 'It's business o' me own I have in the village.'

'Ye dirty...' shouted Deegan.

'Keep that for yer wife,' called Mrs. Dillon from the boundary gate. 'Come on Larry. Ye better hurry up.'

Deegan went home and told his wife. He added to the incident considerably, and the family held a council on the matter. It was decided not to send Deegan after the summons. Instead of that, Mrs. Deegan went out into a field where Macanasa's sons were working and she made friends with them on the spot.

'The Dillons,' she said, 'are in his house and they carried off a box. It must be money is in it and they're taking it to the bank.'

By midday the whole neighbourhood were discussing the matter. The excitement grew intense when Dillon was seen going towards the village in the afternoon in his cart. They also saw Mrs. Dillon come back alone to Lawless's cottage; and an old woman from across the river, a distant cousin of the family, had been brought to Dillon's house to look after the children.

Lawless was not to be seen. After his early walk in the morning he had not left the house. In their conversations, the people now spoke of him with fear.

Dr. Stevens had gone to bed after meeting Macanasa. He did not awake until the afternoon. Then his landlady told him all the gossip. He smiled when he heard it. Then he mounted his bicycle and rode down into the village. He didn't return until after sunset and immediately crossed the river to visit Lawless. He had been drinking. That was apparent by his furious pace, his erect gait and his manner of carrying his hands, not stuck as usual in his pockets but swinging by his sides.

When he reached the black gate, he paused and listened. There was conversation in the house and in the mingling of voices he distinguished Lawless's voice talking rapidly, persuasively, while Mrs. Dillon's voice, slightly hoarse, protested. There was silence for a few moments. Then he heard a loud cry:

'Light! Light! Light! This is light eternal.'

Stevens opened the gate and walked in. The gate creaked as it opened and then banged as it shut again behind him. Somebody in the house rushed to the door and closed it. When he reached the door he heard footsteps darting through the bedroom and into the kitchen beyond. He lifted the latch and entered the sitting-room. Lawless spoke from the bedroom.

'Who is there?' he said.

'It is I, Stevens.'

'What do you want?'

'I want to talk to you.'

'Go away. I don't want to be disturbed.'

Stevens laughed. 'I can quite understand that,' he said. 'Quite.'

He walked into the room and looked about him. Now there were several seats in it; not chairs but boxes with covers on them; evidently brought in from the trunk in the kitchen by Mrs. Dillon. The room was very tidy and there was a lamp hanging on the wall. It was not lit, however, although the room was already quite dark. On the hearth there was a fire lit but it had almost gone out. He waited for Lawless to come in, but there was dead silence. Then suddenly Lawless spoke again.

'Even a dog has pity,' he said. 'Have you none?'

'Why should I pity you?' said Stevens coldly. 'You do not pity me. You are a parasite.'

Stevens heard a rustling sound. He ran to the door and looked out. He thought he saw something disappear to the left around the corner of the house. Then he heard a stone fall from the fence and the thud of something heavy falling into the field beyond.

'Ha,' he said. 'She's gone.'

Lawless came out of the bedroom. He was in a dreadful state of excitement; not hysterical but exhausted. Yet he spoke calmly. 'Why do *you* pursue me?'

'I want to talk to *you*.'

'Sit down,' said Lawless. 'You have been drinking.'

Stevens pulled a seat near the fire. 'Would you like a drink?'

Lawless shook his head. 'I have injured nobody. Yet even here I am pursued. I thought that in this wilderness there would be nothing between me and the light, but like dogs after prey they come, closer and closer. Who are you?' he cried tensely, in a whisper.

'I met Dillon down in the village. He is drunk. He probably won't get home tonight. He had a lot of money with him. He told me you gave it to him. Rather a funny bargain from what I could gather.'

'He told you, did he?'

'Yes. There was no reason for him to hide it, was there? He didn't steal it, did he?'

'No,' said Lawless. 'I gave it to him. I had some money left. It was no use to me. But I thought it might act as a barrier. To keep away the dogs while I pursue the light.'

'Light! I heard you use that word a few minutes ago... To you I suppose I am one of the dogs.'

Lawless went out of the room and came back with his stool. He sat down in the corner of the hearth. 'Tell me why you pursue me?'

'You flatter yourself.'

'Then what do you want?'

'For a moment I thought you knew something and I got afraid. But now I am convinced that you are a humbug.'

'Then why not go away and leave me in peace?' said Lawless. 'See, I speak to you gently, although voices cry out within me and soon I know that I will have power sufficient to raze cities.'

'Then you believe in yourself?'

'I do not believe. It is no longer necessary. I know.'

'And I know that you have seduced this woman into your house for your pleasure. You have preyed on her husband's greed to buy him off. And you jabber to me like a street preacher.'

'Go in peace,' said Lawless. 'The time is not yet ripe.'

Stevens got excited. 'Why don't you talk to me as man to man?' he cried. 'I am a fool to lose control over myself this way. Damn you, you a crazy fanatic, a charlatan. Don't look at me in that silly way. Yesterday you attacked me. Why do you sit there now smiling like a fool? Do you want to fight?'

'I don't want to fight you. You can no longer harm me.'

'You think I am drunk.'

Lawless did not reply. Stevens got to his feet as if to go. But he sat down again.

'You're a clever fellow after all,' he said in a different tone. 'I should have known that. You know you have an advantage over me.'

They both became silent. Lawless began to get restless. 'Why don't you go your way,' he said, 'and leave me in peace? Through her I am going to soar into some hitherto unsuspected form of consciousness. And when two forces meet there is an explosion.'

'Just mania born of lust.'

'It is no lust. For it is not she I love. I realise myself through her. Her presence brings into life all the potentialities of my being, all of it.'

'Has she given herself to you yet?'

'You have a coarse mind.'

'You dare to speak to me like that after buying a woman and her husband?'

'In your soul you know that you lie.'

'I see. She has not given herself to you yet. Until then you can mock me. But afterwards my turn will come.'

'What do you mean?'

'You hypocrite! I suspected you from the beginning.'

'I'm not going to lose my temper with you, but please don't refer to her again.'

'Her! I see. A point of honour. Already she has become a goddess. Do you remember in Gogol's 'Dead Souls' the gay lieutenant that gathered roses, what was it, women of course; he didn't even draw the line at peasant women.'

'You are deliberately trying to provoke me.'

'Yes. I'm trying to break the spell. I'm going to tear the veil of sanctity from you. That is important for me. I've pursued her too, though without success.'

Lawless started. Stevens leaned over and said: 'I was not pursuing God in her. I was just endeavouring to satisfy my flesh. I am a clod, you see, unlike you, I am just a mass of flesh and blood, a damned soul if there is truth in you: but there is no truth in you, and I am not damned, and when I have exploded you like a squib I'll live again comfortably and satisfy my flesh. It's pleasant to talk like this, especially for me, who have shut myself up under a cloak because I was born a slave, the son of a clod, with all the superstition of a clod.'

Lawless became very still. Stevens continued: 'We are an accursed race, like the ancient Jews. There is that same mark of slavery on our brow. We are born in hatred and we live like fanatics seeking God. Why can't we become rich and pompous, and love luxury and find joy in fornication and all the forms of lechery that other races imbibe into their systems with their mother's milk. No. We rush from a house of sin howling in terror lest a bolt might fall from Heaven on us.'

He paused and looked at Lawless curiously. 'You were born free, but we have dragged you down and we'll suck your blood because you have trodden on us for centuries.' He got to his feet again and wiped his forehead with a handkerchief. 'Won't you light that lamp?'

Lawless made no movement. Stevens struck a match and lit the lamp. He sat down again. He began to smile.

'You know, in many ways, you and I are very much alike,' he said. 'The only difference is that my father was a peasant and yours was a landowner. I'm a serf's son, and you are a lord's son. So we pursue God differently. I am out to kill the fellow and you are out to reform Him. But for each of us God is a terrible reality and we can't escape Him. I am honest about it. I humble myself. I acknowledge that I am a clod that will one day disintegrate in death. I acknowledge that I am weaker than my fellows in the struggle for the satisfaction of human lusts, and I hide here, pretending to be happy, watching other people live. But you. You are a pernicious humbug. You think *you* are God.'

Lawless spoke at last. 'I understand you now. Yes.' He reached out his hand and touched Stevens on the shoulder. Stevens shuddered. 'Yesterday I said we were like two sheep hiding from a storm. The storm has terrified one and she hides her head in the grass, refusing to raise her eyes to the safe shelter that lies beyond a difficult path. She prefers to die without effort rather than struggle towards the light. The first blast overwhelmed her. And her weak nature not only suffers her own destruction but also tries to effect the destruction of her comrade.'

'I see,' said Stevens sarcastically. 'You are trying to emulate Christ. That is an interesting parable. The parable of the two sheep. But why not two rams that destroyed one another quarrelling over a ewe? That would be closer to the reality.'

'Yes, even that,' continued Lawless softly but in an exalted tone, 'has the breath of eternal life, when breathed upon by an infinite love. But you must relinquish the earth. Leave the earth and soar. I have just learned to soar. Not like a bird but like a soul in the ancient myths. I am nearly ready, just moored by a slender string and when all is consummated that string breaks and for me the universe becomes my kingdom and I the first man to charter with my mind all its confines. But go away,' he cried suddenly, 'I want to be alone. This must remain my secret.'

Stevens laughed. He took out a cigarette and lit it. Lawless's eyes glittered and he wrung his hands.

'Are you going?' he whispered.

Stevens inhaled smoke rapidly. He looked at Lawless. 'I once had a dream, too. Would you care to hear it?'

Lawless shook his head.

'You must, I want to confess this dream. I have had it here,' he touched his breast, 'for ten years. Wouldn't you like to hear it? Did you ever have the ambition to be a good citizen, to marry and raise a family? Did you ever love a woman so much that the very consciousness of her existence made the world full of laughter and gave you strength to tear up mountains from their beds? Made you soft and credulous as a fool? Eh? Were you ever a human being in other words?'

Lawless began to tap his teeth with the back of his hand and seemed to be utterly indifferent. Stevens became more excited.

'That is the state where man approaches most closely to being a God,' he cried. 'And I once had that happiness. I loved. Christ! How I loved! I was so young and ambitious. And I had treasured my strength like a miser, because I was born poor, and I had to struggle. Then I fell in love. Do you hear? Here is a man, no longer I, because I, as I sit here, am a humbug like you. I am an eyesore, a dying fire. That was a man, of the sort that builds empires and makes Gods, a miserly fellow, a devil for work, scattering none of his seed carelessly, twenty-five, respected for his achievements, just qualified as a doctor, searching about him for some place to dig and build a house, tense with passion, fresh like a new flower. What are you compared to that? A skinny corpse with a madman's mind, raving of universes. Bah! '

'Greed,' said Lawless, nodding his head, as if with a gesture of his reason he had swept aside this temptation of a devil.

'That man found a woman whom he thought a glorious mate. She had that beauty which only grows in Ireland, a sense of purity, like a flower after rain. Her voice was like the music of a fountain. Christ! There could be no evil in such beauty. She was reared by nuns. Do you hear? Her people were rich.'

'Yes. Greed,' said Lawless.

'Wait, you fool. I didn't want her money. I only want to show... I felt sure she returned my love. We became engaged. I intended going to Vienna. I had a theory that.... then one night at a dance, she wore a beautiful dress. There was drink, of course. After the dance, she whispered to me in the cab as I took her home, "Let us go": and it seemed that something foul had entered the world, with her voice. Half drunk, I seized her. We went to my flat, and vices which had hitherto filled me with horror, mad, mad, without shame, everything cracked and toppled down, till afterwards she laughed with her hair streaming about her face. I forced a confession from her. She was twenty-two then, but a priest, a workman, a bookmaker and her father's doctor had been intimate with her. Who else? God knows. But what mattered to me. Furious like some brute stallion I went limp, became a squeezed rag. She went home whispering, the same voice like a fountain. I never saw her again. And after that I became what you see now, a snarling cur, too weary even to snarl until you came here. I.... I am a great man. I have patented an invention. Did you ever hear of it? And now I have another still more foolish. A lozenge. Sometimes I even believe myself. And I forget that I once knew reality and happiness. But I am going to drag you down with me, I'll expose you, you clown.'

'Go in peace,' said Lawless. 'You have suffered for your greed.'

'Are you really God,' sneered Stevens, 'that you can wash away the sins of the world?'

Lawless got to his feet. He raised his right hand.

'Sit down,' cried Stevens. 'Don't look at me like that. This world is a mockery. Let us mock. Mock. Eat my lozenges. Come, worm. Sit down and drink with me. Hey! Hey! Your eyes shine with lust. Last night I was afraid, watching by your bed. Like the centurion I wanted to thrust my spear into your wounds. But now I smell you as I would smell a rutting deer. You are a fool as I am a clod. And I'll laugh over your grave and live after you for I see death in your crazy eyes.'

'Go now,' said Lawless in a calm whisper. 'See the night is silent around you. All nature is asleep. Listen. Everything is at peace. Why must you sneer amidst all this loveliness? Bow down and kiss the earth. Ask nothing and you shall receive everything. For all that is great in man comes without asking. It comes with that madness which some call lust. All great men hitherto have gone out in search of Golden Fleeces. And you were drowned in despair because you think man is but an insect, like the ant or bee, a cog in a social wheel, a builder of hives and hills. Listen to the night, and think that there are innumerable earths and a firmament, loot for our taking. Listen. There is no sound. Listen.'

Stevens stood up trembling. He felt that Lawless towered over him. He also became convinced, now, for the first time, that Lawless was insane, a monster gifted with some unknown power. He felt himself standing on the brink of chaos, with the man's upraised hand dragging him on, off the reeling earth. He tried to cry out. He made no sound.

'Listen,' continued the soft voice. 'This earth is old and weary. Our footsteps have trodden it bare. Why should we waste our genius propping it up like a falling tenement? Here there are no more lands to conquer and life has become as common as the air itself. Like a grain of sand in a desert is man, among so many million crawling things. But up there is unknown space. See how the eyes of man have turned towards it for many centuries. I raise my eyes and crave, crave for power to ravish that space. I am like a sentinel watching for a sign to lead the conquering human army into that heavenly wilderness, from sun to sun conquering. Go. Leave me in peace and wait. Fear nothing if you really love truth and immortality. But if you are the devil...' He stopped and stared at Stevens.

In the silence they heard the sound of rumbling cartwheels and a man's voice singing. Dillon was coming home drunk.

'Yes, I'm going now,' said Stevens, moving towards the door. 'Before I go, I beg you for the last time to clear out of here before you do infinite harm. I am an agnostic and a fool. But I still am human. Before you came, these poor people were living their lives, miserable I own, but happy according to their lights. Before you have done with them it will be a different story. As you say, life is cheap, for you, but each man's life is precious to him, and until we know the truth each one of us has the moral instinct to help preserve the lives of our brothers. Dillon is a wretched fellow and a degenerate man, but still he is human. Listen to him now. Hear him sing. You have done that. Look out, Lawless, or you'll find his knife in your back. I tried to use his wife, I admit, but then I am only a clod. But I did not buy him.'

'I refuse to defend myself,' said Lawless. 'I don't want, at this hour to worry with affairs of...'

Stevens looked back at the door. Lawless had his arms crossed on his breast. He was staring in front of him. Stevens felt an extraordinary hatred of him. And yet as he walked towards the gate he thought: 'He looks just like Christ.'

CHAPTER XV

That night nobody came to visit the Dillons. Dillon came home quite drunk. His cart was loaded with purchases. His wife pulled him off the cart and began to question him eagerly. But he could only mutter.

His wife beat him and put him to bed. In bed he still kept muttering: 'Dr. Stevens said this is a queer business. The land and hundred and thirty quid for.... you he said......' Then he fell asleep.

Next morning, however, he assisted his wife to carry the purchases over to Lawless's cottage. There was a large bed, a table, chairs, linen and food. When they arrived with the first load they found the goats in the sitting-room fouling the place and bleating, waiting to be milked. Lawless was in bed. He asked them to come into his bedroom, in a weak voice. Mrs. Dillon entered the room while her husband drove out the goats. He was lying on his back, looking pale and emaciated. His hair was matted with perspiration. His eyes were strained and bloodshot. He stretched out his hand towards her. She approached slowly, terrified of him. But unconsciously she put out her hand and touched his. His hand was quite cold.

'Something came last night,' he whispered. 'Don't leave me again.'

'God between us and harm.'

'Come closer,' he whispered, drawing her towards him.

She started and pulled away her hand. She went into the kitchen, got the milk can and brought it out into the yard to her husband.

'Milk them goats, Larry,' she said. She waited until he began to milk the goats. Then she went back to Lawless. This time she sat on the edge of the bed and put her hand on his forehead. He put out his two hands and stroked her shoulders. Then he suddenly raised himself and clasped her violently in his arms.

'Don't,' she whispered, 'for God's sake, sir. My husband. He's milking the goats in the yard.'

He did not desist but tried to draw her down towards him.

'Wait a moment,' she whispered. 'Wait till he goes.'

He loosed her then, sank backward and closed his eyes. He was trembling. She went out.

'Larry,' she said, 'when you have the goats milked go for the rest of the things. He's sick.'

'What's the matter with him?'

She did not reply. He finished milking the goats, gave her the milk and went away. She went back to the bedroom.

'Did you take ill during the night?' she said.

Lawless opened his eyes. 'I saw the devil.'

Mrs. Dillon crossed herself and drew away from the bed.

'Come here,' he whispered. 'Give me your hand. Don't leave me.'

'You must be quiet, though,' she gave him her hand and sat on the side of the bed again.

He put her hand to his forehead. It was coarse and red with work but he looked upon it ravenously. She began to shiver. 'What was it you saw?'

'It came several times. I heard a moaning sound pass the window. I rushed out and a white figure passed out the gate. Several times. A moaning sound and a white figure.'

'Were you awake? Maybe it was a dream?'

'No, I was awake. I didn't sleep.'

She looked at him cautiously. Their eyes met. Then some wild feeling took possession of them both. She threw herself upon him, mumbling, kissing his head which she gripped firmly between her hands.

Then after a few moments she uttered a cry and jumped to her feet. He tried to rise after her but she thrust him back.

'God in Heaven look down on me,' she said. 'You drive me out of my mind. Your eyes go through me.'

All morning, Mrs. Dillon and her husband worked in the cottage, installing the new furniture and making it comfortable. It seemed that it was no longer to be the hermitage of an anchorite but something vaguely resembling 'an abode of love'. At least Lawless kept murmuring something to that effect, as his two attendants went to and fro. After a while he got out of bed and took some nourishment, sitting by the fire in the sitting-room. The day was slightly chilly, as there was a heavy mist and some rain. About eleven o'clock everything had been put in its place within the house. Then Mrs. Dillon sent her husband home for some tools to begin working on the yard to clear away the weeds and offal that had gathered there. She herself took a pot of paint and began painting the door outside. Lawless, sitting by the fire, watched her in silence.

Then suddenly Larry Dillon came running back, shouting as he came.

'The priest,' he cried. 'The priest is coming.'

Mrs. Dillon immediately gathered her paint-pot and brush and ran off to the kitchen with them. Her husband came running in the gate. Lawless came to the door.

'What has happened?' he said.

'The priest,' said Dillon, with his cap in his hand. 'He's up on the road.'

Lawless looked up towards the road. Everything was dim through the mist, but he could distinguish, at a distance, half-way up the mountain-side, the black figure of a motorcar and some people standing near it.

'Macanasa is up there,' said Dillon, 'and Deegan's wife.'

Mrs. Dillon came running out of the kitchen.

'Come on home, Larry,' she said. 'We'll be back again, sir,' she said to Lawless.

Before Lawless could recover from his surprise at the suddenness of the affair, the two of them had fled around the corner of the cottage and disappeared. The two goats came out of an old shed where they had been hiding from the rain. Delighted to see him, they came up to be fondled. He paid no attention to them. He went into the house, closed the door and looked out of the window.

He felt very tired. He began to think rapidly. He became aware that something was wrong inside him. As in a nightmare, it seemed that a terrible disaster lay just ahead. Storms of thought came. He was being surrounded. He was alone. The house lifted up into the air and fell down again with a great crash. He died and came to life again. He seized the woman and possessed her. She fled. He became God and swallowed the approaching black priest. He stretched out his hands and laid waste the valley. There was a pause and utter silence. He smelt the falling rain.

Then he seemed to become paralysed. As it were, his body became a block of stone and nothing moved in it but his brain, which worked distinctly, making a sound like a machine, whirring at an extraordinary speed. Down through the green field, where there was a ruined cabin, beyond the marsh, the priest was advancing, whirling a short stick, while a man and woman walked behind him gesticulating. They approached, people of a monstrous size, and behind them tramped a phantom host, myriads of beings, bearing black banners, from all lands, from all the corners of the earth, this host of invisible enemies came, like a great wave of the sea, upon whose frothing white crest the black priest rode like a colossus, brandishing his stick.

Rigid, he opposed this menace and he formed words with his mind to address the advancing host. With his mind he sent out the words, calling on the people to revolt and rend the black priest limb from limb. But the words also froze. They made no sound. Their wings drooped, and although they fluttered out into the drizzling rain, they soon fell and became raindrops. He could smell them falling softly on the sun-parched earth with a soothing sound, a weary gesture of truth fading into nothing before the advancing horde of superstition.

His body grew lax. He saw the priest halt beyond the stream and dismiss the man and woman, who had been whispering to him and making gestures with their upraised hands. The priest's face was dark with fear and what had been great and menacing became small and weak. In this dark, terror-stricken visage he saw the suffering and ignorance of humanity. And the great host of people now approached him not as enemies but as terrified children coming to their father for help.

And he became exalted. The pride of godliness grew strong in him. His flesh tingled with an amorous passion and around his feet he heard the chatter of innumerable children begotten of his fruitful loins. Out of him flowed an endless stream of child begetting seed. He became the father of the universe.

The priest was entering by the black gate.

With a shock Lawless stepped back from the window. The priest coughed. Lawless walked to the door and threw it open. The priest advanced up the yard slowly with his eyes on the ground. Lawless retreated from the door and sat down in front of the fire. The priest coughed again and rapped on the door again urgently with his stick. Lawless neither moved, spoke nor made a sign. Sitting upright, gaunt, hairy, like a rain-bedraggled animal, he yet looked majestic; as solemn and serene as an emperor or man-god, the tomb of an unshakable belief; with blooded hands, nailed, pierced with javelins, torn by lions, gibbeted in a village marketplace, spat upon by harlots in a city's taverns; a ghoul with the lure of God in his eyes he sat in silence.

CHAPTER XVI

'Good morning,' said the priest. Lawless then looked up. He had never seen the priest before. The strange, dark face, with its overhanging dark brows and primitive eyes, startled him. In the first glance, for a minute fraction of time, he saw a wolfish glare in the priest's black eyes: the cunning, fleeting glance of an animal on the prowl. Then the expression became human and sad.

'What have you come to see?' said Lawless gently.

The priest's eyes opened wide. He raised his hands slightly and gripped his short stick. Out of the corner of his right eye Lawless glanced at the stick, noted the silver band below the hoop and the iron ferrule stained with mud. Then he looked up again to the priest's face. They were like two swordsmen feinting for a thrust, fighting with their eyes and the pretended slight movements of their bodies. Then the priest spoke.

'Why do you live like a pig?' he said.

Lawless looked amazed into the priest's black eyes. 'Sit down.' The priest changed his attitude. With a rapid movement he pulled a seat close to Lawless's stool, and, sitting opposite him, he took off his hat, unbuttoned his black raincoat and clasped his hands on his breast. He did not drop the stick, however, but held it between his body and his crossed hands. 'Will you answer my question?' he repeated harshly. 'Why do you live like a pig?'

Lawless was suddenly overcome by a feeling of intense melancholy and looking into the fire, he replied: 'All this is so futile and such a waste of time.'

'What are you talking about?' said the priest furiously. He had evidently expected that Lawless's attitude would be different. Lawless, on the other hand, drooped more and more, sinking back into himself, like a monk lost in the mystic contemplation of his God. The priest brutally caught him by the shoulder and shook him.

'No fooling,' said the priest. 'I'm responsible to God for these people.'

Lawless looked up slowly, with open lips and wondering eyes. 'You are a strange fellow. A priest. What do you preach? Christianity?'

'Don't be sarcastic with me,' muttered the priest. 'Your sarcasm has no effect. I have dealt with fellows like you before. There is only one way to deal with you. Unfortunately the law does not allow.... does not allow us to deal with you in that way.'

Lawless smiled. 'When your hand touched me,' he said slowly, 'it seemed to me that you had been touching me for thousands of years. You thought you touched me in anger, but it was not so. You touched me in fear. Whither am I flying and will you be left behind? That is what your touch said. On your breast you wear a silver cross. You have exposed it so that I might see the image of Him who was crucified by your hands thousands of years ago. I smell the priestly incense from your body. Human sacrifice. And in your eyes I see the image of some forlorn devil's soul, bleared with despair. All this is wearisome to my spirit. There are thousands of years and thousands of hands weighing me down.'

The priest's eyes sparkled. 'There is no use going on like that,' he said curtly. '... Pull yourself together, man. Nobody, no matter how degraded, can sink into this state,' he made a circular gesture with his hands, 'without some spark of manliness left in him. You don't belong to my faith, but, however...' He flushed. 'I know this is a very delicate point, but representations have been made to me. I am responsible to God for these people. I am sorry for your own sake, but you are outside my jurisdiction. Certain definite, very definite, representations have been made to me by members of my congregation.'

'Your congregation?' said Lawless, becoming alert.

'Yes. You have been tampering with them,' continued the priest. 'This must stop.'

'Explain yourself.'

'You know very well you have been playing the old game of the proselytiser here. We thought we had finished with all that. First you tried to bribe them by letting their cattle graze on your land. Now, failing that, you give money to this wretched couple. You buy a man and woman, body and soul. More body than soul,' he added with a sneer.

Lawless rested his chin on his hands.

'I hear everything,' cried the priest in a loud voice. 'I am responsible to God for these people. I know this has been going on. There are others here, too. All this rubbish about people going to die no more, your indecent conduct standing naked in the river. Deliberate incitement to the most foul sensual abandonment. Go your way, sir. If you must satisfy your base passions, you must do it elsewhere. I am responsible...'

Lawless touched the priest's knee with the tips of his fingers.

'Lay your soul bare to me,' he said gently. 'Then perhaps we shall talk not in anger but like brothers, seeking the great hidden secret.'

The priest drew back.

'What do you fear?' whispered Lawless.

'I fear God,' said the priest with scornful emphasis. 'It would be well for you if you feared God this day.'

'Why do you fear God?' whispered Lawless.

'Eh?' The priest became nervous. 'I fear God because... because I am a sinner.'

'How have you sinned, brother?'

The priest started and drew his dark eyebrows down over his eyes. The eyes roamed back and forth over Lawless's face shrewdly.

'I see,' he said. 'That's your game.'

Lawless looked back gently, inscrutably. The situation became very tense. The priest tapped the ground with his stick.

'I don't want to argue with you,' he said coldly, but with a great effort that the words trembled as they issued.

'No,' said Lawless. 'I thought not. You fear me as you fear God because you are a sinner. By your own mouth you have confessed. A beast of prey, swollen with offal, you have come into the wilderness armed with a club to stamp out my fire.'

'You are taking a very dangerous line,' said the priest slowly. He grew rigid and tapped the ground still more.

Suddenly Lawless drew himself up and his eyes flashed: 'You wretch. There was once a great seer who loved so much that he destroyed an Empire with his love. He inflamed slaves and harlots with the fire of his divine holiness. He set the world ablaze. But you have stamped out HIS fire. And wherever a seer arises you come like dogs after prey to stamp out their fires. See. In your hands you carry a club. And in your eyes there glows the fire of savage greed. And on your breast you carry the curse of your fathers. The cross of Him who was crucified for thirty pieces of silver. Once humanity stood on the threshold of Heaven, while a great man battered at the door, carrying the banner of eternal light and you dragged him back and nailed him to a Cross and plunged humanity into two thousand years of darkness. Again man is weary of his tomb, and he is trying to push aside the door of his sepulchre. There is a mighty murmur over all the land from sea to sea. I stand here alone in the mountains and I hear their groans, heaving up against the weight of iniquity that has accumulated upon them. Priests, usurers and all the lechers; that lick the sores of emperors. Their cry is tearing my soul asunder and again all shall be lost unless one man shall batter down the door. Dark-eyed carrier of clubs, I am that man.'

'I see,' said the priest coldly, getting to his feet.

He raised his stick and stood over Lawless. The stick shivered in his trembling hand. Again Lawless watched the stick out of the corner of his eye with a curious cunning. But he did not flinch. His chest swelled out arrogantly like a male fowl preening itself before a mate, showing its voluptuous contours. It rustles its tail and gurgles in its throat and swells with amorous passion, while she lowers her head and arranges her feathers.

He might have struck had not the two goats appeared at the door, side by side, and gazed into the room with their melancholy yellow eyes at the two men, one sitting and watching, one standing in an uncouth attitude with an upraised stick. What pantomime was this? The goats watched, chewing their cud and shook the drops of dewy rain from their hairy bodies. They tapped the floor with their dainty hoofs as they shook. They smelt the men and wondered with their eyes and chewed their cud.

The priest turned on the goats and beat them out into the yard with his stick. Indifferent to him, they playfully laid their tails along their backs and began to toss their heads at him. He returned to his seat.

'I see,' he said again. 'You are beyond reason. It's... it's this degrading passion of love. That's the root of it.'

Lawless screwed up his eyes.

'Well,' said the priest, 'we'll see who is going to win. You or I. You're looking for trouble and you'll get it. Mark my words. So you are going to save humanity. That's an old story. You're not mad, though. I see through you all right. It's corruption that is at the bottom of it. I suppose you were a failure at everything and now you have a clever idea in your head that you can start some fake religion to make a little money out of it. Eh? Why didn't ye stay in the city where ye belong, among the lazy women in the suburbs who have no way to satisfy their jaded sensuality, but gazing into bowls and table tipping and every other abortion. These poor people... It's hard enough to keep them on the straight path as it is, their poverty and misery. I'm not going to argue about religion with you. Might as well try to talk reason to a pig, as to one of you people. Blasphemer! The walls of the Church are too strong for your blasphemy. If I had my way it's on a hot grid-iron... Knock the nonsense out of you. You degraded ruffian. How could I appeal to reason with a man like you?'

Lawless sat still. The priest's face became contorted with an extraordinary sort of expression. He seemed to be drawn in spite of himself under the influence of the gaunt, hairy, bedraggled man opposite him. The arrogance left his voice, and, though he continued to talk in a loud angry tone, he appealed instead of denouncing.

'All this talk about revolt,' he said. 'It's an impudent lie to say that there is any religious impulse behind it. False doctrines and the vanity of scientists, artists and pagan poets. These are the beginning and the end of revolution. It begins in lust, and it will meet its destruction in lust. Don't delude yourself, my good man. We are watching these saviours of the people. Give unto Caesar. If you went tomorrow into any village in Ireland and talked this nonsense in a public place, they'd tear you to pieces, so they would. Anti-Christ. You are the man, you say. I'm a sinner, am I? But I hold the keys. I have the key to salvation. My job is hard enough without your making it harder for me. You're not as.... Come now... You're not entirely perverted. Won't you talk reason? Won't you listen to reason?' The priest laid his stick on the ground. 'Did you ever think of the hour of death?' he said in that soft voice with which priests both charm and terrify delinquent members of their congregations.

'Yes,' said Lawless quietly. 'I have thought of death.'

'And what do you think is going to happen to you when you face your Maker?'

'I am not going to die,' said Lawless.

'You are still bent on playing the humbug.'

'Very well,' said Lawless, after a pause, 'Go in peace.'

The priest did not move. 'When did this idea get hold of you?'

'Since I ceased to fear God.'

'So you believe in God?'

'That is my secret.'

'I see... Come man, do you realise what you are saying?'

'What have I said?'

'Eh?' shouted the priest, so suddenly and in such a loud voice that he himself was startled. Lawless remained perfectly calm. Out of the corner of his eye, he glanced at the stick which now lay on the floor. His pose was that of a woman who is being interrogated about some dangerous secret. There was a faint look of glee in his eye. His lashes dropped and his whole body had a suggestion of subtle grace that was most aggravating to the priest. Yet the *actual* expression of his face was one of dour ecstasy. 'You have dropped your club,' he said. 'Now you too can become God. Do you know that every man is a God, and that every living thing is a god, and that these instruments of oppression, these cowardly emblems of fear kill with their touch the breath of divinity. You don't know.'

'I see,' said the priest. 'A pantheist. That stale rubbish.'

'No,' said Lawless. 'I am not anything for which man has yet found a name. For man is only just beginning to strive towards a new manhood. And everything that he has inherited is rapidly becoming confused, language, thought and religion. Before a birth there comes a terrible cataclysm. The womb is rent and cries of pain are heard. Terror seizes the mass. And but a few are sustained by a vision of what is to come. A voice is heard, louder and more sweet than any voice that has spoken hitherto. I am that voice.'

'Are you a Communist?'

'I told you that I am something for which mankind has not yet found a name. But some time they will give me a name, although...' He turned towards the priest and frowned. 'You are terribly unhappy,' he said. 'Many things have become clear to me looking at your face. Strange, indeed. Your dark face has caused a greater love to possess my soul and a greater brightness to enlarge my mind. True it is that man can only conceive happiness by the contemplation of unhappiness. Here now,' he cried in a singing voice, 'here, at this very moment, here all is clear and I can tell you what I am and why I am and what man is to me. And I can tell you what you are and what you are to be. Now all is clear to me, gazing at your dark, unhappy eyes, in which I see myself as I was wandering in darkness, a tired soul, listening in fear to the moaning of the wind and to the waves of the sea. Everywhere I heard the warnings of living things that death is near and that no man knows eternity. When cocks crew on silent summer days I feared. When I saw a mother lose her child in death, I feared, and the despair in her forlorn eyes was my despair confronted with this horrible mystery. In darkness I came here, wandering from among tired and hungry people. From the multitude of crimes and the unhappy throng whose madness terrified me. I had stretched out my hands and raised my voice, preaching universal love and they did not hear, for your club was laid to their backs. Their heads were bowed under the lash and their ears choked with fear of your superstitions. And then I learned here in the wilderness that the chief attribute of love is pride. There can be no love without pride. And there can be no God until man denies the existence of any God outside his own soul. Through loving all things the man-God attains the supreme worship of his own soul, which is the ultimate purpose of his existence and the consummation of his immortality.'

The priest stooped for his stick as Lawless paused for breath. Lawless saw the movement out of the corner of his eye. Although his face had become completely that of a mystic in the ecstasy of a vision, the corner of his eye and his body had the curious, subtle tension of a faun-like she animal, on guard and ready for flight. The face was illuminated by a wild power. The body and the watching eye were remote from the face, more subtle, older yet without age, not human. They neither laugh nor cry, but their eyes gleam with a strange malice and countless races dance to their fairy piping.

The priest picked up the stick and made a slight movement away. He gathered his coat about him and his heavy jaws trembled. His eyes protruded. He too looked powerful.

'Once blood was ugly,' continued Lawless. His voice throbbed. 'Once my soul wept at the thought of flowing blood. But now I rejoice, for it is my blood, and it gushes forth like a fountain from the hearts of slaves and their masters, into a fountain that reaches to the heaven world. Lo! Man is on the march, and I am he who stands in front, beckoning without words, for words have lost their meaning. I am he who bursts first the cord and soars into the heaven world. And the power of my love spreads out over all the world and draws them upwards, bursting their cords. They burst their cords. Their murmur becomes a triumphant shout. Covered with blood they march, trampling on you, club-bearer. Soon, soon, this holocaust shall be made and man shall soar into the heaven world. Conquering man, redeemed from fear by the pride of love. Death shall be routed.'

The priest jumped up and uttered something aloud, hoarse and savage. Lawless arose too, agile, on guard. His face shone.

'Come, now,' he cried. 'Rouse your God and lead him forth. Let me see whether He or I is the mightier. See, can he strike down in death my incorruptible soul. And tell Him that man has at last, through me, uttered the great defiance to His impudence. *We shall not die.*'

The priest rushed out, crushing his black hat down on his shorn skull.

Stepping like a faun, Lawless moved to the window and watched him go. His eyes glittered.

CHAPTER XVII

A crazy man sees in his mind a vision of disordered nature, hears weird speech from the inanimate earth; goes forth naked, uttering wild cries; wanders seeking a quiet place, where he may look upon nothing but darkness. He finds no darkness anywhere but always a red mirage before his sick eyes.

So the priest went forth, muttering aloud: 'What blasphemy! What horrible blasphemy! This is no madman, but Anti-Christ.'

He went out the gate and turned to the left towards Dillon's home. Macanasa and Mrs. Deegan had disappeared. But in the distance figures could be seen outside each house, watching. Rain was falling slightly. Alone, in that queer glen, carrying a short stick, hurrying along a marsh bottom between towering heights, while the soft summer rain fell silently and mournful curlews cried in flight, this holy priest looked most unholy and distraught, a strange demented creature flying from one still more strange and demented who had threatened him with doom.

He crossed the boundary fence in such haste that he fell down at the far side into the wet mud, soiling his black clothes. That further enraged him, and he advanced at a run with his stick held out. The collie bitch saw him coming, and, thinking him a dangerous fellow by his manner, she rushed out to attack him. He pursued her with his stick and as she jumped over the garden fence to escape, he threw the stick after her. Larry Dillon ran out of the house bareheaded and drove off the dog with stones. Then he fetched the stick to the priest, who stood in the yard panting. The priest took the stick, paused, drew in a deep breath and then clutched Dillon by the throat.

'Father,' said Larry Dillon.

The priest raised the stick and glanced all round him. The dog, which had come hovering about, uttered a loud yelp and fled. Mrs. Dillon came to the door of the cottage with the younger child in her arms. The child howled, seeing the priest. Mrs. Dillon called out. The old woman who had come to look after the children, came out of a byre, and dropping a pail of water into the dung, she raised her hands and shouted something which was both a prayer and a curse. Larry Dillon, clutched by the throat, let his body droop and kept whimpering: 'Father. Father.'

The priest swung the stick and struck with great force. He loosed Dillon's throat. Dillon sank to the ground and grasped the priest's legs. He did not cry out or moan or wriggle about, but remained still, with his hips raised and his legs stiff, like a soldier doing gymnastic exercises and afraid to move before the word of command. The priest went on striking him on the back.

Then Mrs. Dillon came forward slowly, holding the child in her arms. She stared in silence. Her dark hair was about her face. Her lips curled. She seemed to watch the beating with interest, and it was hard to say whether the hatred in her countenance was directed against her husband or against the priest. She seemed to watch the rising and falling stick, not the two men. However, when she was beside the priest, she said in a low, tense voice: 'Ye better stop that, Father Raverty.'

The priest looked at her. At that moment the old woman also came forward as fast as she could. 'Give me the child,' she said, stretching out her hands. At the same time she glanced furtively at the priest. The priest flushed. He understood that the old woman was afraid that even the wife was in danger and that perhaps the child might get hurt.

'Yes,' he said, unconsciously expressing his thoughts aloud. 'I've a good mind to do that too.'

'Keep back, Nelly,' said Mrs. Dillon to the old woman.

Larry Dillon raised his head, let go the priest's legs and crawled away. He got to his feet. Mrs. Dillon stared in a strange, cold manner at the priest, as if she were thinking of something entirely remote from what was happening.

'There now,' she said. 'Have ye done what ye wanted to do, ye brute?'

The priest became very embarrassed. His anger still blazed in his countenance, but he was so ashamed of the presence of the squalling child and of the old woman that he was dumb and helpless.

'That's what you are,' continued Mrs. Dillon coldly. 'A brute. And from this day let there be a curse on you for bringing shame on me before the whole world.'

'Father, don't mind her,' said Larry Dillon. 'Stories were brought to ye, Father, that weren't true. It's on account of Mr. Lawless, Father, that ye —'

'Don't mention that man's name,' shouted the priest, suddenly becoming possessed once more by the same fury.

'You... you've been taking bribes.'

'Shut up, Larry,' said Mrs. Dillon in a low voice. 'Go into the house an' wipe the dirt off your face. I'll talk to him.'

'Don't mind her, Father,' said Larry Dillon once more.

'You're both equally bad,' cried the priest in a more restrained voice. 'Look at your house. Look at the condition of that child. Look at the state you are in yourselves. Ruin all round me. You idle ruffians. It's in a house like this that temptation is received with open arms. But you'll be sorry for it. I thought we had done with this long ago, selling yourselves, body and soul.'

'Aye,' said Mrs. Dillon coldly. 'That's fine talk. An' who did we sell ourselves to, may I ask? Not to you, I know; for ye wouldn't give the smell of a hot potato to a dog. Who did we sell ourselves to?'

'It was all on the square, Father,' said Larry Dillon in a cringing voice. 'I was talked into it though.'

'What are you talking about, ye slave?' cried Mrs. Dillon, becoming angry. 'D'ye want to disgrace me more an' you after lyin' there while he bate ye with a stick?'

'Now, the peace o' God be on ye,' began the old woman, and won't ye —' She did not finish what she wanted to say because the other child appeared at the door and began to cry. The old woman ran towards it and took it into the house.

'I have a right to earn me livin' what way I please,' said Mrs. Dillon to the priest, 'and you can't stop me.'

'I'm responsible to God for your immortal soul,' said the priest, 'and –'

'Faith, ye can make yer mind easy on that score,' she retorted. 'From this day I'm finished with ye. Ye can curse an' damn, for all I care. For if there is a God it's on you His vengeance'll fall and not on me that's living in misery an' hardship all me life. What have ye come here for, only to take the bread out of our mouths? Yer more concerned with yer own pocket than with immortal souls.'

'Don't listen to her, Father,' said Larry Dillon. 'This is how it was.'

'Go on,' she cried, again becoming apparently indifferent. 'Lie down like a dog before him.'

The priest was trembling with anger, but he kept thinking. 'I'm afraid I've gone too far. The bishop is sure to hear of this. '

'He made a bargain with us, Father,' said Larry Dillon, 'an' it was all on the square, as far as I could see, till Dr. Stevens began to talk to me about it.'

'He's another o' them,' said Mrs. Dillon.

'Will ye let me talk now, woman?' said Larry Dillon.

'Him with his smutty lozenges,' mumbled Mrs. Dillon.

'Go on,' said the priest. He looked curiously at Mrs. Dillon. He had not heard her last remark properly.

'Herself was to look after the house,' continued Larry Dillon. 'Tend and cook... well, he said that he wouldn't be long before he.... something queer he said, anyway. And after that, he said, whatever was going to happen, the land was to be ours. There was money given, hundred and thirty pounds. He gave it into our hands, 'cause he said he had no use for it and it would be the same as wages. Well, if he lived, ye see, as he might do, Lord look down on us, for years, it's a poor way to wish any man harm, what with rummagin' around and journeys to the village I'd have to make for groceries and clothes an' that I counted it up over a number of years, we'd be at a loss for the hundred and thirty –'

''T wouldn't take ye many weeks to drink it, not to mind years,' interrupted Mrs. Dillon.

'So, only for the land,' continued Larry Dillon, 'we'd be at a loss. An' then he arranged I was to buy the things outa that. It all came to twenty-three pounds four an' eightpence out of twenty-five pounds. There is the remainder of it there in me pocket, Father, bar a few bob I drank in Geraghty's.' He held out some money. 'Herself has the rest put away. I bought a bed an' things. The house beyond was in an awful state.'

He stopped.

'Well?' said the priest.

'It was Dr. Stevens put it into me mind, Father,' continued Larry Dillon after a short pause, 'that there might be something wrong in it. So I didn't ask Mr. Gillan, the solicitor, to come up, same as I was told. He said to have a document drawn up. I thought it was all on the square.'

Mrs. Dillon took a pace forward. She put the child on her hip brushed back her hair off her forehead and said bitterly to the priest : 'And what d'ye make o' that now?'

The priest looked at her. 'What dealings have you had with this man?' he said in a low voice.

'What man?' she said.

He pointed towards Lawless's house with his stick and pursed up his lips.

She looked and lowered her eyelashes. 'Yer wastin' yer time, if yer tryin' any o' them stunts on me. I'm sick an' tired of this life.' She turned around and walked away two paces. Then she stopped and turned again. She said in a distraught voice: 'Is it any pleasure for ye to be torturin' poor people like us? Isn't it punishment enough for us to be livin' in this misery without yer comin' to torture us more? D'ye think ye can turn me against that man with yer double meanin' looks and yer smutty mind? He's the only honest man I ever came across. He's the only man that ever spoke to me kindly or put the love o' God in me heart, an' I'm not goin' to listen to you sayin' anything against him, for I can see through ye. There was a time when I was afraid o' ye, but that day is gone, both for me an' for many another in this country. Aye! Ye may do yer dare and yer damnedest, but yer not goin' to prevent me from workin' for that man that's holier than the Pope o' Rome an' God's holy angels in Heaven. I'll tell it right out here now, to you Father Raverty, and to you Larry, that I don't care from this day, what becomes o' me, but I'm goin' me own way an' I'm goin' to be content in me mind for me mind is made up.' She looked at the priest, spat and muttered an obscene word.

'Aw, Father,' whispered Larry Dillon, 'Don't mind her. Don't mind her.'

'I warn you,' shouted the priest hoarsely, shaking his stick at Mrs. Dillon.

She moved away to the door swinging her hips.

'Keep away from that house,' he cried.

She turned at the door, spat and entered the house. The priest rapped the ground with his stick. Dillon came up to him.

'Don't be hard on us, Father,' he said.

'Now, I'm warning you,' the priest told him. 'Keep away from that house and keep your wife away from it. And see that she returns the money, too. I heard blasphemy in that house today from that man's lips, such as... Give that money back at once and never speak to that man again. I'm warning you. I'm responsible to god...'

He walked away. Dillon followed him, running along sideways near the priest's left shoulder and stammering.

As the priest went out over the broken down wicket gate, Dillon suddenly cried in a fawning voice: 'Ye were forgettin' about yer dues, Father. Here it is.'

He pulled out of his pocket some silver and copper coins, the change which he had previously shown; the remainder of the money his wife had given him to make purchases.

'I drank a few bob in Geraghty's,' he said. 'God forgive me for it. Whatever is over the dues say a Mass for my soul for it, Father.'

The priest walked on some distance while Dillon ran after him sideways offering the money. Dillon became terribly excited, fearing that the priest would not take the money. 'Take it, Father, and forgive us,' he kept saying.

Finally he grew bold with fear. He seized the priest's hand and pressed the money into it. The priest's fingers closed on the money. The priest moved on with the money gripped in his hand. He did not speak or look at Dillon, but moved on hurriedly with the money in his hand.

Dillon halted and looked after the priest. When the priest was about to climb over the boundary fence into Lawless's land he slipped the money casually into his trousers pocket. Then Dillon put on his hat and slouched back towards his home. His wife was standing in the doorway with her arms folded on her breast. She stared at him. Her eyes mocked. There was a cruel smile on her face. He stopped and said:

'What are ye lookin' at me like that for?'

She said nothing, but went on smiling at him in a cruel way. He tried to go past her into the house. She would not let him pass. Then she stopped smiling and said: 'Larry, you'll take notice of what I say, not of what *he* says. D'ye hear? I'd twist the head on yer neck so I would.'

Then she stepped aside. He entered the house. She went out to the fence of the haggard and watched the priest's progress through the glen. She stayed there for two hours watching, under the shade of a tree. She saw the priest moving about from house to house at a furious pace. She saw him talk to people. She could not hear him, but she knew by instinct what he was saying. He was giving orders for a boycott. She didn't care.

And at last she saw him climb the mountain slope to his motor car. She heard the engine start. The sound carried all over the glen. Then it rushed away as if announcing by its joyous roar to the glen dwellers that it was grateful for their gift of petrol money.

When the car had disappeared, Mrs. Dillon still remained looking over the fence, under the shade of a tree. Her lashes drooped. A passionate look came into her face. She was now looking towards Lawless's house.

She was dreaming wild dreams.

CHAPTER XVIII

After the priest's departure Lawless had a slight stroke. He was standing by the window, learning forward, smiling joyously at the discomfiture of the priest who was running away. He was feeling very happy. His body felt young and irresponsible. His blood was warm and coursing freely through his veins, as when a young man is playing a dangerous prank and rejoices in the danger. His mind was gay too, and conscious now of the wild flight it had a few minutes before. He was dimly aware that his mind had created something great and beautiful a few minutes before, and now he was laughing softly at what he had created; or rather at what he had become a few minutes before. He was looking out the window from the corner of his eye, as he had looked at the stick, laughing at the other fellow, who had terrified the priest with beautiful words.

Then something appeared to tap him lightly on the back. He straightened himself, stopped smiling and listened. His head, his fingers, toes, gradually became cold. He moved backwards quickly, gasped and reached out with his two hands to catch something. He kept going backwards until he reached the far wall. Then he turned to the left and tried to rush to a seat near the fire. The muscles of his legs became rigid as he moved forward. He stumbled several times and then fell on to the seat. He was cold all over now. He sat very still and waited.

He had a sensation as if his blood were leaving his body, evaporating. While this was happening, his head reeled, became confused and momentarily everything swam before his eyes. His body was dead and his mind had loosed itself from his head. He was weighed down with enormous weights. His mouth got afraid and began an incredibly fast movement with the lips, as of an animal running at a great speed. But with a gesture of his mind he stopped it. He contemplated himself in peace. He meditated on the question: Am I dead?

In answer to this question the powerful personality who had fought the priest with beautiful words rose up in him, a heavy limbed fellow, soft of flesh, with luscious lips and loving eyes, hairy, with a brooding mind. His body was very warm and soft with love and it thawed the rigidity. It dispelled the fear. The mocking eyes disappeared before it. The malicious joy became a thing of shame and in its place there came the power of large boned giants, who flop across the land, across rocks with large feet, grinding bones, roaring above the noise of storms.

He stood up and felt his body large about him. He felt he could swing his hips like a woman, swagger like an athlete, thrust out his chest and grip heavy weights lightly with his hands. His mind saw crowds of people gazing up at his lofty height. They became women. Then he bowed his right arm and clicked his tongue: 'My beauty,' he said.

His luscious lips were moist and he blubbered over the words. He felt so passionate that its sensation completely intoxicated him and he breathed heavily, making a singing sound. He sat down again, stretched out his legs and hands limply and closed his eyes. He became his normal size again. His mind grew active and he thought of the priest with his stick warning her not to come near him. Would she come back?

He began to speak aloud. 'What is immortality now? What is the power of an ocean to the power of my desire? I have burst the dam and the flood is overwhelming cities.' He laughed foolishly. Then his face grew stern. He exerted himself to call her to him. He leaned his chin on his hands and kept calling her: 'Come, come to me. I want you. I stake everything on this last throw. Everything in the balance. Come. Let me ravish you. Come.'

Time passed, in waves, slowly. His eyes grew tired. His thoughts grew more and more abandoned, chaotic. But his desire did not grow less in spite of the weariness that overcame his body. It became transformed and he transformed her in his thoughts into various exotic forms, winged and four-footed, bodyless, many-bodied. His body remained still and expectant, reserving its force; but his mind ravished her in countless ways and reproduced itself endlessly with greater vigour and freshness after each assault.

The light grew dim. Night was falling. The goats bleated loudly in the doorway, demanding attention. And yet she had not come. But he went on calling her in his mind, heeding nothing else. Neither hunger nor thirst troubled him.

She came at last. He heard her open the gate and he knew it was she by the way she closed it stealthily. He also recognised her steps coming along the yard. The goats saw her. They ran out bleating. She did not enter by the sittingroom door but went off towards the kitchen, followed by the goats. He sat still. Presently he heard her milk the goats. He felt hungry. He got to his feet and began to move around the room.

After a while he looked out the door. The goats were milked. They had mounted the roof of the shed and were standing there side by side, eating the bark of a laurel bush that grew beside the roof.

At last she came in brusquely. 'Sorry, sir,' she said in a coarse voice. 'There was a bit o' trouble. I couldn't come back to give ye yer dinner. I'll get it for ye now, sir.'

'Don't cook anything,' he said. 'Give me some milk and... are there any eggs?'

'Yes, sir.'

'And honey? Did you get honey?'

'Yes, sir.'

'Everything raw,' he said. 'Two eggs, raw. Honey, bread, milk. That will be very nice. Won't you have some with me?'

'I'll get it ready now,' she said, without answering him.

She put a cloth on the table and brought the food. He began to eat. He pressed her to join him, but she refused and went off to the kitchen. He ate a hearty meal. And not until he had finished did he notice that her attitude towards him had changed. He called her. She entered the room, coming around from the kitchen through the yard.

'Yes, sir,' she said.

He smiled at her and said nothing.

'Oh! God!' she cried suddenly. She sat down near the fire and threw her apron over her head. She rocked herself.

Lawless folded his arms and watched. Then he caught himself smiling, covered his mouth with his left hand and held up his right hand. He struck his forehead. 'I, too, should groan.'

She dropped her apron and looked at him curiously. There were tears in her eyes. 'What's that, sir?'

He looked at her wildly. She shuddered and drew back.

'Sit still. You are unprepared and so am I. So we are both disturbed. What has disturbed you?'

'I don't understand, sir,' she said.

He sat down beside her. 'Look into the fire and tell me. Let us be quiet.'

'The fire is gone out.' She rose suddenly.

'Let it be,' he said, gripping her arm and forcing her back into her seat. 'We can both look at the dead fire. It is better to think over a dead fire. What has disturbed you?'

'It was the priest, sir.'

'Listen. Don't call me sir. Call me father. Will you?'

'Why is that, sir?'

'No, not sir. Father.'

She opened her eyes wide and looked at him frankly for the first time. His face looked wonderfully handsome. The eyes were smiling and the smile dispelled the strange look of fanaticism which sometimes made his face terrifying. She smiled, showing her teeth. Their gaze became rapt. Their smile became fixed. Both together held their breath. Their lips moved. Then he said softly: 'I humble myself before you. I embrace all in you; all. Call me beloved. And I shall call you beloved. Beloved!'

She stopped smiling and furrowed her forehead. 'I'm afraid.'

Their faces were very close together.

'What do you fear?'

'I don't know what I'm afraid of now,' she said slowly. 'A little while ago it was something else, people I felt were watching. But now... I don't know what it is. It's something else. I'm not afraid of him, now. Not a bit. Only, it's the same as in the chapel, when the sun is shining on the statue of the Blessed Virgin.' She sighed. Her eyes wandered over his face.

He touched the crown of her head with his right hand. 'You feel terribly lonely. You feel there is a great wide...'

'Yes, yes,' she interrupted. 'I don't... How could I call you be – what you said. I'd be ashamed.... Only one thing I'd... I'd like if you...'

'What would you .... ?'

'You wouldn't think it queer?'

'Tell me.'

She flushed and lowered her head until her forehead touched his knees. Then she turned her head, laid her cheek against his knees and looked up at him seriously, still flushing and timorous.

'Well?'

'I want to kiss your feet,' she said almost inaudibly. 'Then I wouldn't be afraid.'

With a quick movement she threw herself at his feet and embraced them. Then she rose slowly, clinging to his knees, with her head thrown back, smiling. She was very beautiful.

'And now?' he said.

She laughed and drew in a deep breath through her closed teeth. He nodded his head. Raising both hands she caressed his face with them. 'I wanted to touch your face.'

Then she clutched him about the body and laid her head against his breast. Half sobbing, half laughing, she said: 'Now you belong to me. I'm not afraid of you.'

He opened his eyes wide and started. He opened his mouth and looked sideways, and through the window. It was getting dark.

'Don't look like that,' she said. 'I'll call you beloved. Kiss me.'

When their lips parted he said: 'And why not? Take my body as I take your body.'

Her forehead became furrowed and her eyes became suspicious. 'Why do you say that?'

He did not answer for a moment. Then he said: 'Let us wait another little while. Perhaps there are things that I should disclose to you that you may be prepared. For you must understand that this is something that never was before. Something is about to be consummated that may be......' He looked into her eyes. 'No. You are not prepared. Tell me what you expect.'

Again she flushed. 'Oh, sir, don't tease me. You'll make me afraid again.'

'Hush,' he stroked her head. 'Let us be quiet again. There must be no sacrilege. Something is beyond there,' he waved his arm circularly, 'that is... But.... What eyes! '

He looked into her eyes savagely, and then drew back, gritting his teeth. She also gripped his knee until her fingers strained.

There was silence for several moments. Then she suddenly became restless. She said in a whisper: 'I'll soon have to go.'

He almost shouted at her: 'You'll have to go. Where?'

She spoke bitterly: 'What do I care what they do to me? Then why don't I have the courage to face them and stay here if you'd let me stay? But.... I'm listening always to something whispering in my ear, Run for yer life. That's what it says.'

She looked at him. His face had become rapt. She drew back her head with a jerk and said in a different tone, quite cold and almost harsh:

'Father Raverty beat my husband in the yard, in front of the house. Then he threatened us. He went round to all the houses. I know he told them that... I sent the old woman afterwards to Mrs. Mullen for the loan of her washboard and she wouldn't give it. So I know what he said to them. No one'll speak to us now and they'll all be watching us.'

Lawless said nothing. Then she continued: 'Larry, that's my husband, he went on his knees and asked me for God's sake not to come near this house, and to bring back the money—'

'What money?' interrupted Lawless.

'The money you gave us. The priest said it was a bribe.' She looked at him shrewdly.

'I.... I,' began Lawless. 'Of course. Oh! Let us forget that. I should have told you that.... You *see* I didn't know until today that our association would be on another plane. But why must you go? All this has now become remote and of no consequence. Burn the money. Why must you go?'

Her face became still more cold and harsh. 'Don't you see? I'll have to be careful. I'm supposed to just come over, do me work here and then hurry back. I told Larry. I said to him: "Do what ye like. Take a pound an' go into the village. Then, maybe, ye'll feel better." But he wouldn't budge. He's sitting in the house now.'

Lawless leaned his chin against his hands. He looked at her strangely. 'Do you want to turn back?' he said in a deep, trembling voice.

'What's that, sir?' she said, changing her mood. She became tender again.

'Listen,' he said, putting his hands on her shoulders. 'Look me in the eyes. Look at me.'

She looked into his eyes, shuddered and closed her eyes. 'Your eyes go through me,' she whispered.

'Look, look,' he said, excitedly. He raised her head and held her face close to his with his hands against her cheeks, until his breath was on her lips as he spoke. 'Do you not see something you have never seen before?' he said eagerly. 'Don't you feel something incomprehensible and vast beyond your imagination? Something standing on the borderland? Don't you see God in a mirage just beyond the edge, where you might stretch out your hand and touch his Being? Don't you?'

'I don't understand what you are saying,' she whispered. 'I love you.'

'You love me,' he continued. 'That is good. Then soar with me. You do. Don't you? Looking into my eyes you lose sight of everything else. You fear nothing. Is that not so?'

She nodded and fondled his shirt at the breast with her fingers.

'And you often longed for something,' he said. 'Something you couldn't name or understand. You' were waiting.'

She sobbed and put her arms around his waist. 'God! I'm going to faint.'

'Hush,' he said. 'In darkness and stillness and silent watching our souls will unite and then eternal light is born of their infinite humility. They have ceased to see and have ceased to hope. For death nor sorrow can touch them because they have ceased to be themselves and have become infinite. Who are we now, beloved? We do not know. And already we do not know who we have been. I a king and you a queen or two slaves lashed by a master. What matter who we were? Nothing *is* now. Nothing *must* be until we are transformed, you whom I have chosen and I whom man has chosen. Listen,' he cried in a wild tone, as he raised her head again and gripped her cheeks, 'don't you feel you are far from here?'

She nodded her head weakly, sobbing. She was very pale.

'Yes,' he cried. 'It is so, beloved. What word?' He listened. Then he embraced her furiously and she lay in his arms, lifelessly. He looked away, meditated, and then uttered an exclamation. She shuddered in his arms. He staggered to his feet, holding her drooping body in his arms. He looked about him. Then his eyes flashed and he moved off towards the bedroom door.

Suddenly she became rigid and said: 'Let me go. Quick.'

He dropped her and she caught him by the arm. 'Listen!'

Somebody was outside, moving cautiously along the grass of the yard. She caught his head in her hands and kissed him fiercely on the lips. 'I'll be back in the morning.'

She put her hand to his mouth to silence him. 'I hope you'll have a good night's rest, sir,' she said, going to the door.

He took a pace forward and then halted as he heard her say: 'Is that you, Larry?'

'Yes, it's the little fellah cut his finger,' said her husband in a querulous voice. 'I came over to see could ye get a bit o' stickin' plaster.'

'Oh! God!' she said. 'Something is always.happening.'

'What's that?' said Lawless, coming to the door.

Larry Dillon was outside twirling his hat in his hand.

'It's nothing, sir,' he said in a fawning voice, 'only the child cut his finger. I hope I didn't disturb ye?'

Mrs. Dillon ran off towards the gate. 'Good-night, sir,' she said. 'Come on, Larry. I can't leave the house a minute but something has to happen.'

Her husband lingered outside the door twirling his hat. When his wife had gone out the gate, he said to Lawless: 'I wish ye'd get someone else, sir.'

Lawless came out and stood beside him.

'That money is on me conscience,' said Dillon.

Lawless took another pace forward and stared at Dillon.

'The priest was sayin' that it wasn't right,' continued Dillon. 'She has got it, sir, and she won't part with it.'

Lawless walked past him with his hands folded on his chest. 'What is this man to me?' he muttered.

Dillon followed him slowly. They both went out the gate.

'Listen, sir,' said Dillon.

Lawless halted by the little stream.

'I do be thinkin' a lot, sir,' said Dillon in an awed tone. 'An' maybe you're right, but it's the way other people see things that things have to be done. You don't take it bad of me?'

Lawless looked at him and muttered to himself. He crossed the little stream. Dillon followed him. Suddenly Dillon grew angry and raised his voice. Halting, he thrust his hat on to his head and said in a furious manner: 'God's curse on ye anyway, ye have me ruined! '

Lawless, walking ahead, looked back and said, scowling: 'I don't know you. Be gone.'

Dillon went off running and calling back: 'May the divil sweep ye. Ye have me ruined.'

Lawless mounted the great rock and drew in the air into his lungs. Then he stretched his arms over his head and felt the cold night wind play about his body. It was very dark. The rain had ceased but the sky was covered with black clouds. The mountains were like clouds, too, dark masses. It was terrifying.

For a long time he stood motionless with his arms stretched out. Gradually his body grew colder. He became afraid of the mountains and of the dark sky crowding about him. He lowered his arms at last and turned up the collar of his shirt. He was just wearing, as usual, a shirt and trousers. He felt the cold. Then he felt an aching pain all over his body.

Thinking quite normally, he wondered whether he had caught a chill. But soon he associated it with his desire for her. And now this desire was altogether repugnant and sordid. He was amazed at this. He was still more amazed to find himself feeling pity for her husband, and then at finding himself, in his imagination, walking with her husband to some unknown place, hand in hand, whispering together, both in tears. Then he thought suddenly: 'The whole project is foolish.'

'What project?' he said aloud.

He jumped from the rock and began to run through the gorse. He circled the house. He halted by a fence and thought: 'I'll walk quietly in the night. I am alone here now. Sweet, sweet, lonely night, you are my day, for likeness strives towards likeness and your colour is the colour of my soul waiting in anguish for what the morrow will bring. Near or far, bright or dark, what shall be my tomorrow?'

Then he felt there was someone watching him.

He walked about all night.

CHAPTER XIX

When day broke he entered the house and went to bed. He fell into a sound sleep. When he awoke she was standing by his bed. She had his breakfast on a tray. She was smiling at him. She had put a bright comb in her hair. Her hair was dressed in an arch over her forehead, parted in the middle, a black glossy mound with the bright comb glistening at the rear. She had rings on her fingers. There was a sensual look in her brilliant black eyes. Her lips trembled with excitement. Her bosom heaved. Her lithe body was poised as for a spring. Her white teeth bared as she smiled. She looked cruel, triumphant.

He had been calmed by his sound sleep. When he opened his eyes and looked at her, it was with the feeling of repugnance which the thought of his love for her inspired in him during the night. Seeing her cruel smile and the way she had adorned herself with trinkets, he thought: 'There is no virtue in her nor in me.'

Then her beauty hypnotised him, stirred him up, made his blood throb and his eyes grow dim. He felt lured by her smile. She caressed his head and he could feel the passion of her touch. She spoke to him. He felt that her voice trilled. It rang clear and musical like the voice of a young girl. She had, indeed, become transformed during the night, but not as he had hoped.

Raising himself on his elbow, he looked at her with wonder in his eyes, and he thought: 'What do I expect of this? This is no sister soul.'

Coldly now, with remorse, he saw his vision as that of a deranged mind, dreaming of an impossible godliness, detached from earth and flesh and the insatiable lusts that bring death with the satisfaction of desire. He saw her as a she beast, caressing him with velvet paws, with white teeth bared to suck his blood.

He rose up in bed, violently angry. His face became as cruel as hers. He smiled too. But when his hands touched her, it was not in anger that he pressed her to him. All thoughts vanished but one, the desire to caress her.

She put aside the tray. They lay together, and as he held her in his arms, a glorious dream of conquest flashed through his mind. Then he rejoiced in her cruelty and in his own likeness to her. He felt as proud as the angel who had defied Jehovah. Strength, wisdom and beauty became his attributes. And he floated towards her, with her, through radiant worlds, while the air thundered its applause.

But soon a mocking voice sounded louder than the thunder of the air, and he grew weary of his flight. His mind grew numb. He heard her speak afar off. He listened to her. Every word fell into his ears heavy and meaningless. He never answered her. She kissed his lips, and her kisses burnt him. He closed his eyes. Then she too lay still beside him. He fell asleep again. When he awoke she had gone. He paid no attention to her absence, because now it seemed that he had no desire for anything.

He dressed and wandered round the house listlessly, standing still at times as in a dream, then walking about, touching things and murmuring. He went into the little room where there were books, the human skull on the table and the picture on the wall. He touched the skull, smiled and threw it into a corner. It meant nothing now. Several times he went to the outer door and looked out. He wanted to go into the warm air and walk beneath the trees by the river, to listen to the rumble and the running water and to bathe his feet in it. But there were people abroad and animals and birds. There were insects in the grass. Even the sun itself looked down on him. And it was abhorrent to him to be seen by anything but her.

At midday she came again. They began to talk now.

'I'm goin' to get into trouble over this,' she said.

He did not reply. Now, when he was near her, he could say nothing. He had to put his arms around her and beg for her favours. She resisted his advances and spoke to him in a coarse, harsh voice.

'I saw Larry talkin' to old Macanasa,' she said. Lawless did not reply.

'I forgot to tell ye,' she said, 'that he got up last night and went out. He was out a long time.'

Lawless started.

'Who is that?' he said.

'Larry.'

'Your husband?'

'Yes.'

'Ha!' he said. 'I thought there was somebody following me all night.'

'And where were you?'

'I was walking about.'

She mused. Then she became tender. 'Why is that?'

He didn't answer. She put her arms about him.

'Are ye fond of me? Honour bright. Are ye?'

He said nothing.

'Hey,' she said suddenly. 'Would ye take me outa this? Would ye run away with me? You've been in foreign countries, haven't ye?'

Lawless moved away from her and covered his face with his hands. She said no more, but cooked some food for him. Then she went away.

During the afternoon he saw her husband pass the gate three times, and he became greatly afraid. But in the evening, when she came again, he abandoned himself to his love for her, and they spent the time until night fell loving one another, whispering and saying strange things. And again she went away, leaving him desolate and disturbed. Again he went out and walked about. Now he was watching to catch somebody following him. There was somebody, but it proved to be old Macanasa, who was going about examining rabbit traps. Lawless passed quite close to the old man who said something, but went off hurriedly without replying.

In this way day followed day rapidly. He was now completely cut off from human intercourse except through her. She brought him fresh news every day. Every day she became different. According to her, a catastrophe was imminent. Now she referred to her husband as 'He.' She called Macanasa 'the old codger'. These two men were the central figures in the horrid nightmare that she wove. They were always whispering together. Her husband was becoming distraught. He refused his food. He wept at times. He made long rambling speeches about money that was on his conscience. And most terrible of all, he was weaving a rope of horsehair. On the fourth day, she said that Dr. Stevens had been into her house the previous night and that he was going into the city with some new discovery he had made. 'Them smutty lozenges he's goin' to patent.' On the sixth day she reported that the priest had delivered a violent sermon in the chapel and that the whole parish was 'talking about it'. A policeman had spoken to the glen dwellers after Mass.

These conversations made no impression on Lawless. He had fallen into a stupor regarding everything but her. He was always watching her, always hoping that this 'last gamble' would help him at last 'to batter down the door'. But every day she became more remote from what he had hoped she would become, and in spite of that, he became more and more her slave.

Now the idea of flight was always before her mind. She continually suggested it to him. Her expression grew harder. 'I don't even care about the children,' she said. 'I'll leave them with him if ye like. Only... he wouldn't look after them. Is it on account of the children ye don't want to come?'

At last, one evening she became violent and shouted at him. 'D'ye think,' she cried, 'I'm goin' to spend me life here foolin' around with ye? God Almighty, can't ye be a man? Take me outa this an' I'll keep ye meself if ye can't work? If ye won't come I'll go alone. I can't stand this any longer. He has that rope finished now. I'm afraid to sleep in the house for fear he'd choke me in me sleep. What are ye goin' to do?'

Then on the twelfth day of their intimacy, she came running to the house in the morning with her dress torn, crying out: 'I'm murdered. He murdered me.'

He jumped out of bed when he heard her coming. She dashed into his bedroom and threw her arms around his neck. She appeared to be in hysterics with fear.

'What is it?' he cried.

'Just when I was leavin' the house, he attacked me. Come on. Hurry! Hide me until we can get away. We'll get away after nightfall. Say you're comin'. Look. He caught me by the breast. I'm bleedin'.'

She staggered over to the bed and sat down. He sat beside her. The sight of her torn dress hurt him so much that he forgot his growing despair of her and of himself. A sudden hope came to him that now, at last, she would understand what he required of her. He embraced her and whispered: 'Listen. What has happened is no misfortune, but...'

She looked up suddenly and interrupted. 'But what?'

He looked into her eyes. Her eyes glistened with tears, were cold and cruel. Still he went on, making a great effort to recover his faith. 'It's a preparation for what is in store for us.'

'I don't know what ye mean,' she scowled.

'We are going to go.'

'God!' she cried in a delighted voice, clasping him in her arms.

'Hush!' He gently pushed her away. 'Not where you mean.'

'Where then?' she said angrily.

He became excited. 'I must tell you now. Come with me up to the highest place on these mountains. There we shall await our transformation.'

'What the hell are ye talking about? Don't ye see the state I'm in?'

'Understand,' he murmured, that I have chosen you to join me in the attempt to do something that will change the whole history of humanity.'

'How?' she said harshly. 'Can't you be quick? What are we to do?'

'Calm yourself and try to understand me.'

'I'm listening.'

'Look into my eyes.'

'Go on, for God's sake. Can't ye see me lookin' at ye?' Her bosom heaved and she curled her lips. His lips began to tremble and he was trying to speak, but no words issued from him. 'Well?' she said with a sneer.

Then she tittered. With a wild movement he clutched her arms. 'Why do you laugh? Do you laugh at me? What do you see in my eyes? Are you a whore or am I ... ? Curse you. Tell me.' He lowered his voice and spoke tenderly. 'Forgive me. Listen. Let me say just a little... No, don't draw back. Listen. Don't you hear the thunder of the universe calling us?'

She laughed outright and pushed him away. She got to her feet. Then she hissed at him: 'A bloody madman. That's what you are. O! God! Just because you were born a gentleman I made a toe rag of meself for ye. Listening all these weeks to yer damn rubbish. You an' yer universes. Go up the mountain with you?' She spat. 'No, then. It's not up I'm goin', but down into the city an' no man is ever goin' to get me again except for cash.' She drew her shawl over her disordered bosom and tossed her head.

He threw himself face downwards on the bed and cried aloud: 'Desolation! Desolation!'

'Howl, ye bloody madman,' she jeered at him. 'An' ye can rot here now in the dirt I found ye in, until they throw ye into a lunatic asylum. Look at me, says he. As if that beardy tramp was anything to look at. Who d'ye think ye are? God Almighty?'

Lawless jumped to his feet, stood erect and threw back his head: 'Yes,' he said. 'I am God.'

She paused for a few moments. Then she laughed, took a pace towards him and cracked her fingers in his face. 'Take that then from me if ye are. An' ye may warm the biggest fire ye have in hell for me, but it'll be a day or two yet before I get there. In the meantime......' She leaned forward, whispered in his face, laughed and walked hurriedly out of the room into the sitting room. 'Ha! So you're here, too.'

Lawless started and ran to the door. He saw Larry Dillon leaning against the outer entrance. His wife faced him.

'Forgive me,' he said to her. 'Me temper got the better of me.'

He looked at Lawless. He held out his right hand: 'Oh! sir,' he said in a despairing voice, 'can't ye see what ye have done to me?'

Lawless came forward. 'Out, out! Be gone, both of you.'

Dillon caught his wife by the arm. 'Come on away.'

'I'm goin' farther than ye think,' she pushed past him out the door.

'Stay,' said Lawless, rushing to follow her.

Dillon stood in his way and held up his hand. 'Don't you touch her, sir. You have no right to her.'

Mrs. Dillon turned towards them in the yard. 'Now, I hope ye cut one another's throats. I'm going.'

'Where are ye goin'?' asked her husband.

'Where am I goin'?' she said cunningly. 'Where do ye think? I'm goin' into the city to lay a charge of attempted murder against you.'

She walked rapidly to the gate. Her husband ran after her, appealing to her. They went out the gate. Lawless sat down on the threshold of the door and began to mutter to himself: 'Desolation, desolation, desolation!'

CHAPTER XX

He sat on the threshold wearily listening to the departing sounds. Her voice was the last sound he heard, loud and clear, in laughter. For a long time after it had ceased, her mocking laughter still re-echoed in his mind. It rang like a wild bird's scream carried on a gale over a thundering sea. And it seemed to say: 'Arise and follow me'.

He tried to rise when the wild mocking sound ceased to ring and jingle in his mind. He could not move. His limbs were helpless. Then the terror of old age possessed him; the horror that old men feel when their palsied hands fumble helplessly with a weight they had gaily tossed about in youth. The horrid, lean thighs and yellow lips of death.

He looked about him furtively, like a hunted animal. He saw the fence, the gate, the trees, the mountainside. They were all there still. They had not changed. But there were blossoms no longer on the hawthorn bushes. The feathery arch of white blossoms had gone. The bushes were laden with fruit. He said aloud: 'Time has passed. Death is approaching the earth. I hear his wings rustling. Now indeed desolation surrounds me. She has sucked me dry and left me.'

He listened again. Everything was still, as still as death. Not a sound or thought broke the death-like union of his mind and nature. A cunning look came into his eyes. His lips trembled, opened and broke into a smile. He raised his hands and clapped them together. He jumped to his feet. A malicious joy rooted out all consciousness of the past. He went into the house and entered the bedroom. He saw the bed on which she had sat a little while ago. He thought she was still there at first. He approached the bed gaily, with outstretched arms. Then his arms folded aimlessly about the empty air where his sick eyes had seen her figure. As if he had been mortally stabbed, his body crumbled down upon the bed. He tossed about and rose again, reeling drunkenly. His lips were set. His eyes glared. He tore at his shaggy head and then grasped his shirt and tried to tear it from his breast. But his hands were weak. He leaned his head on his shoulder and staggered away heavily into the kitchen.

The two goats had pushed open the outer door and they were looting the food. They paid no heed to him. He approached the unicorn and tried to fondle her, but she rushed out the door. The other goat followed her. He shuddered and stood erect.

'What?' he cried aloud. 'Am I defeated by a woman?'

He opened his eyes wide and stared in horror at the floor. 'No,' he murmured. 'Not a woman. All have become possessed of devils. Even these animals. Quick.'

He closed the kitchen door and locked it on the inside. Then he hurried into the sitting room to close the other door. But just as he reached it, he saw the old man, Patrick Macanasa, standing outside in the yard, resting his two hands on his stick. The old man touched his hat and said: 'Good morning, Mr. Lawless. Praise be to God, the weather looks none too good for the hay. Are ye afraid o' thunder?'

'Ha!' said Lawless. 'You have come again.'

'Yes, yer honour,' said Macanasa. 'It's only a little thing that brought me.' He spat and then approached a few steps.

'Why not?' said Lawless to himself. 'Perhaps I had better surrender.' 'Come in,' he said aloud.

'No, I won't be comin' in,' said the old man. 'It's only a word I wanted to say.'

'Come in, come in,' said Lawless, retiring into the house.

Waiting inside the door, he thought: 'He has done this to me. Let him have the land that he covets. Then perhaps he may ...'

Still the old man did not enter. Lawless went out again into the doorway. The old man was standing a few paces away with his two hands on his stick.

'Why don't you come in?' said Lawless eagerly.

The old man spat again. 'I see yer goats isn't milked yet this morning,' he said.

Lawless then became aware that the goats were standing together to the left bleating loudly.

'Why won't you enter the house?' he said again.

'Well,' said the old man, 'maybe if I told you why, that ye might take it bad of me.'

'Nothing could be worse than what is,' said Lawless. 'What is your reason?'

'Well,' said the old man cunningly, 'it was how I thought you might be thinking of leavin' the place.'

His shrewd eyes searched Lawless's face. Lawless did not reply.

'There's trouble beyond,' said the old man, pointing with his stick towards Dillon's house.

Lawless looked and moved his lips.

'She's goin',' whispered the old man.

'Where?' said Lawless.

'And where would she be goin'? Sure it would be hard to say where an elegant woman like her 'd be goin', leavin' house an' home. An' who'll look after ye, Mr. Lawless now that she's gone?'

'You want something,' said Lawless eagerly. 'Take what you want.'

'Sure I can't take what's given already.'

'My money do you mean?'

'Money is like water. Put it in the river an' it flows to the sea. Put it in a bucket an' it's swallowed by the sun.'

Lawless turned and went into the house again.

'Are you coming in?' he said.

Macanasa came to the door and put in his head. 'Is it in the name o' God yer askin' me?'

'You are afraid,' said Lawless. 'Then it was you did it.'

'Done what, yer honour?'

'At all costs I must get rid of you.'

'Ha!' said the old man, stepping back. 'What's that ye say? Is it murder yer after?'

'No, no.' Lawless came forward. 'I mean no harm. I'm going soon.'

'An' where would ye be goin'?'

Lawless suddenly got angry. He stepped out into the yard. 'You herd of gluttonous swine,' he cried. 'You were offered the universe and you could only see the acorns in the earth's mud. Woe to me the day I pitied you. For how could beauty grow from such a putrid root? I'm going now and you can have this barren place. But if any of you try to prevent me... Beware.'

The old man said nothing for a little while. Lawless waited. Then the old man spoke: 'It's them goats I was thinkin' of. It's a pity to leave animals without care.'

'Take them. I want to be entirely alone.'

'Were ye thinkin' o' goin' away today? There's thunder comin'.'

Suddenly Lawless's eyes became cunning. He leaned against the door post and put his hand to his heart. He groaned. Then he staggered into the house and muttered: 'Help! Help! '

Macanasa came to the door and looked in. 'Dr. Stevens has come back. Will I send him over? Maybe it's medicine ye want.'

'Come in and help me to my bed,' said Lawless.

Macanasa watched him from the door. But he did not enter. 'Dr. Stevens is going away tomorrow,' he said. 'Maybe I'd better send him over.'

Lawless did not reply. The old man retired from the door. Lawless heard him talking to the goats. Then after a while he looked out the window and saw that Macanasa had tethered the goats together and was leading them out of the gate.

'Where are you taking them?' he shouted.

'Over to the house,' said Macanasa. 'Will I leave them?'

'No. Take them,' said Lawless.

'I'll send over Dr. Stevens,' said Macanasa.

Lawless raised his hand and opened his lips to say something but he remained silent. Macanasa went out the gate and closed it behind him. He spat before moving away. Lawless remained at the window. Then a great turmoil arose from the direction of Dillon's house. A cart began to rumble along and people were shouting. He moved away from the window, pulled his stool into the far comer of the room and sat down. The turmoil approached, grew less and then increased. Somebody was weeping aloud. With horror he realised that it was a man who was weeping. Then he recognised the voice. It was Larry Dillon. He stretched out his hands and murmured: 'Brother, brother, in your heart alone has my seed taken root. You alone share with me my grief. Weep with me.' Then he began to shed tears and felt comforted.

The noise was passing his house. He heard her voice again. He could resist no longer having a last look at her. He went to the window and saw her on a cart with her two children and an old woman. Her husband followed the cart, bareheaded, holding the tailboard with one hand and gesticulating with the other. On either side of the cart there were shouting people. They passed upwards. The sounds grew faint. His head swam. He walked away from the window to his stool and sat down again.

Silence! A cock crew. Then a chorus of sad voices murmured softly:

'Rise upon the wind, flapping your long white wings. The earth is growing old.' He closed his eyes and, breathing deeply, he inhaled the fragrance of imaginary flowers, flowers of the heaven world. He was transported to an endless plain, bounded by luminous clouds. Beneath his feet the new earth was radiant with blooming flowers. Flower blossoms floated in the air. Flower petals fell in showers on his head. Each flower had a laughing eye and a triumphant joy spread over the endless plain, the joy of innumerable flowers laughing, blooming, smelling sweetly. Here there was no thought nor change, but the endless motion of never changing beauty.

So he sat still, with closed eyes. Then a stone struck the zinc roof of the house. He started and jumped to his feet. He heard Dillon's voice say: 'It was he done it. He has me ruined. Let me go till I murder him.'

Lawless moved cautiously to the window and looked out. He saw Dillon outside the gate struggling in the arms of two men. Others stood by. Macanasa was there with his two sons. The Deegans were also there, man and wife. There were others whom Lawless had not seen before. The people were arguing violently, but Lawless could not understand what they were saying. The Macanasa came up to Dillon and shook his stick at him. 'Now,' he said, 'ye have the price of yer bigness. D'ye think we don't know that ye have the money in yer pocket an' ye seen takin' it away in a box? And maybe a paper too with the land written down in yer name on it.'

Dillon crossed himself and said: 'I swear by the cross of Christ that she took the money with her, an' it's a black heart ye have, Paddy Macanasa, to bring allegations like that against me. I never touched a cent of it bar three shillings or four. An' any man that says I lay any claim to the land, may he die of thirst.'

Macanasa struck the ground with his stick. 'Well may you say it.' He shook his stick in the air. 'No grabber'll ever drink milk off this land while there's blood in a Macanasa.' He went over to the fence, picked up a stone off the ground and put it on top of the fence, as if taking possession of the house.

'And what did the priest say, may I ask?' said Mrs. Deegan.

'He said a hag's tongue has the devil's mark on it,' said Macanasa. 'I'll let no man harm him till he goes.'

'Where is he goin'?' asked Dillon. 'Let me go, will ye.' He ceased struggling and the too men loosed their hold of him.

'And how could I know where the elegant man 'd be goin'?' said Macanasa.

'Then I'll follow him,' cried Dillon.

Lawless suddenly moved towards the door, murmuring: 'The time has come.'

When he appeared at the door, he raised his hand and said: 'Brothers, come near. I wish to speak to ye.'

'Holy Father!' somebody exclaimed. Then all the people became silent.

'Don't be afraid,' said Lawless. 'Enter the yard and listen to what I say. This is important.'

The people began to whisper. Then Macanasa came forward. He passed in through the gate, took off his hat and made a sort of curtsey. Then he leaned his two hands on his stick. He looked about him in a serious way; but as if he were conscious of playing a part in a game for children. Then the others began to push their way in through the gate. Dillon stood outside until they had all entered. Then he also moved forward muttering. He came forward until he was in front of the others, within a few yards of Lawless. There he folded his arms on his bosom, stood squat and scowled at Lawless. His ragged figure and unshaven face had a dignity that was very unusual. He looked Lawless straight in the face frankly and with the arrogance of a man looking at another who has wronged him. And as Lawless remained silent, he said: 'Now we're here, what have ye got to say? I'm watching ye.'

'It's a shame, poor man,' said a woman in the crowd. 'He looks sick.'

'Stand back there, Larry. Ye've only yerself to blame,' said another.

'Quiet will ye now,' said Macanasa. 'I'm here to protect Mr. Lawless.'

The people became silent. Then Lawless raised his hands slowly and made a movement, as if he were going to float into the air; moving his shoulders forward and raising his chin. 'Soon now,' he said in a singing voice, 'I am going to go from here. The time has arrived for my departure. So I speak to you, that you may know me as I am and not as my enemies have told you that I am, an agent of evil.'

He paused, looked at the sky, glanced furtively at Dillon and continued in a louder voice: 'I am going where none may follow me because none of you are worthy to follow me. But if you do as I bid and tell all men to do as

I bid, some day you may follow me.' He paused again and covered his face with his hands. He trembled. The people looked at one another.

'Poor man,' said one. 'It was a low trick to take advantage of him. They rooked him clean. He's out of his mind with the loss of all he had.'

'Aw, shut up,' said another. 'Can't ye see he's balmy?'

'Silence,' said Macanasa. 'Go ahead, yer honour.'

Macanasa's eyes were twinkling. Lawless uncovered his face and cried in a loud voice: 'I am the spirit of revolt. I have humbled myself before the ugliest and meanest of mankind in order that a great pride might be born in me. I have allowed myself to be stripped naked in order that the baseness of man's ingratitude and the enormity of his greed might be made manifest. I have been imprisoned for my forbearance. I have been ridiculed for my humility. I have been deserted for my love. Now man has taken everything that belonged to my human spirit. I am no longer man. I have revolted.' He paused for breath.

'Well, tell us what ye did to my wife. What about me?' Dillon raised his two hands in a gesture of rage and yelled: 'What about me? Where am I to go after me two children? God in Heaven!'

'Aw! Shut up,' said a man. 'It's like a circus. Can't ye get another wife.'

'Quiet, will ye?' said Mrs. Deegan. 'Can't ye let the poor man have his say?'

'Now hear me well,' continued Lawless slowly. 'And tell men what I say. For although my message may rouse your foolish minds to mockery, other minds will be inspired to challenge death as I go to challenge it. Listen.'

He paused again. Now nobody spoke. All listened intently. He remained silent for a long time, with his right forefinger raised. His face shone. His eyes glittered. Around his eyes there were dark hollows. The pallor of his face against his rank brown beard was horrifying. Yet his body appeared to be powerful and supple, standing taut. He was leaning forward on his right foot. His left leg was pressed backwards rigidly. Then he cried out arrogantly: 'I am going to conquer the universe. I shall pitch my camp within the gates of Heaven and I shall make God my slave. For I am more proud than He. Then I shall send a sign. They shall receive it who make a virtue of pride and defiance.'

He paused. Not a sound was heard. He still remained rigid but his right leg began to tremble violently. Then he said: 'Tell all men that the attributes of immortality are pride and defiance – pride and defiance.'

Suddenly his body became lax. His head drooped forward. He stared at the people. He scanned each face eagerly. As his eyes moved to each face, each face turned aside. Then he dropped his eyes to the ground. The people began to mutter.

'What's he talkin' about?' said one.

'Can't make head or tail of it,' said another.

'Come on away, for God's sake,' said a third. 'This is no place for us. A doctor should be sent for.'

'Aw, leave him alone,' said the first. 'Them fellahs are only kiddin' all the time. He's a bloody cod. All the same, its not fair for them Dillons to rook him the way they did.'

'Hey, look at Larry pretendin' to have his rag out. Its all made up between himself and the wife.'

'God! I never thought of it. Janey, what d'ye think?'

'Sure. He'll be gone tonight after her.'

'Now he can—'

'Wait,' cried Lawless, suddenly raising his head. 'Don't go yet.'

The people became intent once more. Lawless pointed towards the house. 'Take everything,' he cried. 'And this land,' he waved his hands, 'let it be taken by the most defiant.'

'That's me,' cried Macanasa, coming forward. 'Him that has most claim.' He pulled a handkerchief out of his pocket, unrolled it and held out a silver coin. He spat on the coin and held it out to Lawless: 'Here's a luck-penny for it in the presence of witnesses.'

Mrs. Deegan rushed forward. 'Hold on there,' she said. 'Are ye sellin' the land, sir?'

Macanasa pointed his stick at her and said to Lawless: 'An' ye going on yer long dangerous journey, Mr. Lawless, where the divil himself'll be hoofin' it after ye, don't cast yer eyes on a woman.'

Lawless folded his arms and said: 'I no longer own anything on earth. Take what is there and go. Come. Take everything.'

'Then I take the land in the presence of witnesses,' said Macanasa, laying the coin at Lawless's feet.

'The lead-roof robber has done me in,' cried Mrs. Deegan, rushing towards the door.

'Where are ye goin'?' said her husband.

'I'm going to have something for me trouble.' she said, disappearing into the house.

'Come, come, the rest of you,' said Lawless with feverish eagernes. 'Leave nothing. And if any man wishes it, he may take the clothes off my back.'

First one and then another advanced. Gradually they moved forward all together, protesting.

'Where are ye goin'?' one said. 'Surely to God...'

'Keep back there now,' said another. 'Don't make a show o' yerselves and the state the man is in.'

They all talked, protesting, but they all moved forward. Presently they broke into a run and entered the house, pushing one another. Lawless, Dillon and Patrick Macanasa were left alone in the yard. Macanasa picked up the coin from Lawless's feet and pressed it into Lawless's hand. 'Keep it. As the soldiers say when they come back from the war, it'll be a souvenir of a poor old man that'll remember ye in his prayers when ye're gone.' He spat, wiped his mouth with his beard and said: 'God bless yer honour. I always said he were a holy man. Ye're in safe hands now. An' wherever yer goin', nothing can stop ye, for me prayers'll get ye there like a shot off a shovel. Keep that luck-penny now. Is there a pocket in that trousers, savin' yer presence, where ye could stick it in?'

He took the coin from Lawless's unresisting hand and pressed it into the left trousers pocket. There was a loud noise within the house. Lawless, paying no attention to Macanasa, watched Dillon's brooding face.

'Now,' said Macanasa, straightening himself and striking his stick against the ground, 'ye're as safe against the wickedness of man as if the Pope of Rome anointed ye with water from the well of Lourdes. An' every blade of grass that'll grow from this day on the land ye've returned to its rightful owner'll be smilin' up at ye; and you sittin' up there where ye're goin', maybe smokin' American tobacco from a golden pipe. An' drinkin' red wine,' he shouted into Lawless's ear, 'drinkin' red wine out of a cup with jewels on it, greater than any king. That's me prayer for ye. An' I'll go now to see that them people do no more damage. Let me kiss yer honour's hand.' Macanasa stooped down, kissed Lawless's unresisting hand and then moved off towards the house, spitting on his stick.

'Brother,' said Lawless to Dillon, 'why do you stand there?'

Dillon unfolded his arms off his chest: 'I'm watching ye, Mr. Lawless.'

'What do you want?'

'I want me children,' cried Dillon in a fierce, mournful voice.

Lawless started. Then his face darkened and he looked up the mountainside.

'Give me back me children,' shouted Dillon again.

Lawless furrowed his forehead and looked at him. His face was wrinkled with pain.

'I can only give you one thing,' he said.

Dillon gritted his teeth and snarled at him: 'I'm watchin' ye. Ye can't escape me.'

'I won't try to escape you,' said Lawless quietly. 'Perhaps we shall go together.'

'Well, I'll see that you don't have her, anyway,' said Dillon in a whisper.

'Eh?' said Lawless. 'Ah! I had forgotten. Of course... you are her husband. No. I'm not going in that direction. If you still want to follow her, go and leave me. I have forgotten her already.'

Dillon approached. There was a fierce conflict in the house. Somebody was trying to push a table out the door. When Dillon was beside Lawless, he said: 'Wasn't it made up between ye?' he said fiercely. 'Aren't ye goin' to follow her? Didn't ye say now ye were goin'? But ye won't escape me. I'm watchin' ye.'

'Calm yourself,' said Lawless softly. 'I tell you I have forgotten her. I'm going elsewhere.'

'Where?' said Dillon.

Lawless did not answer. Then Dillon moved away. He said as he went: 'I'll be back again and by God ye won't escape me.'

'Mr. Lawless,' said Macanasa, dashing out of the house. 'The house is being wrecked. Stop them barbarians. The house is a part o' the property. Stop them, I say.'

'Yes,' said Lawless. 'Tell them to leave my stool. I may be some hours yet. Perhaps tomorrow.'

Macanasa saw Dillon going out the gate. 'Where is that man goin'?' he said. 'I must look after him.'

He looked into Lawless's face shrewdly. 'There must be no bad luck on a new property,' he said. 'Where blood flows the grass withers. And maybe this day'll be better for travellin' than tomorrow, yer honour. Where are ye goin'?' he shouted after Dillon.

Lawless went into the house. He was jostled in the doorway by Mrs. Deegan, who was coming out backwards carrying the mattress and bedding off the bed. Her husband was coming behind her with the frame of the bed. Lawless was thrust aside against the wall. The Deegans, shouting, burst through the doorway, followed by a tall man who carried two chairs that were badly broken by the struggle to gain possession of them. Shouting, cursing and pushing, the crowd swept out of the house as soon as he appeared. Each carried a load. He saw an old woman carrying the human skull in her shawl and dragging the large oil painting in her hand along the floor. He stood by the wall and watched them move past him. Then he noticed that a young man who was going out had the stool in one hand. He snatched the stool. The young man, not recognising him, tried to hit him with the floor mat which he held rolled under his arm. But instead he hit the person in front of him. They both began to curse and rushed out the door shouting. Lawless went to the fireplace with his stool and sat down.

Again the people pressed into the house to see was there anything else to be taken. They rummaged about and took everything. They even took the tongs off the hearth and the pitcher into which he milked the goats. They left not a single thing in the house except the stool which he had snatched from the young man. Then they moved away with their loot. He heard Macanasa shouting at them in the yard as they went off. Two men began to fight in the yard and the women screamed. Then suddenly the struggle ceased. They had all gone.

'What's happening?' he heard a voice say outside. It was Dr. Stevens.

Lawless began to smile. He laughed aloud and throwing out his hands in front of him he looked at his palms and then closed his fingers slowly over his palms. 'See,' he murmured, 'I hold nothing. Now I have nothing to fear. I am free. He cannot harm me.'

'He's goin', yer honour,' Macanasa was saying to Stevens. 'It's how he's goin' to tramp the roads in his shirt an' trousers. Maybe he's took it into his head to drive cattle to the fairs. And maybe not. Maybe he's goin' somewhere else. But wherever the elegant gentleman is goin' 'twill be easy to follow him, for he leaves the road covered after him with a power of generosity.'

Stevens laughed, a loud, bitter laugh. Then he said in a low mocking, bitter voice: 'So Christ died for you people.'

'Dr. Stevens,' said Macanasa, 'it's a bad habit ye've got into, takin' the name o' the Lord God in vain. But I must be off now again to look after Larry Dillon. He's hearing the noise of the fairy wind in his head with loneliness, for his wife an' children that's gone an' left him. Ye won't stay long with Mr. Lawless, doctor, because he's in a hurry to be gone an' it's better not delay the man wherever he's goin'. For I've to hurry now before the winter comes to tidy the fences on this land an' save the house from ruin, his honour told me an' he sellin' me the place to look after it well. "Look after it well," says he in the presence of witnesses, "an' let it be a credit to me when I'm gone." For the land is the pride of any country, an' who could look after it better than them as has a right to. I'll be goin' now to Larry Dillon. The poor man has met with a bad misfortune. Ah! a bad misfortune.'

Stevens smiled again and shook his head. Then he entered the house, coughing loudly. He saw Lawless sitting by the fire. 'I came to bid you goodbye. It seems we're both going away.'

CHAPTER XXI

Lawless looked up and smiled.

'I knew you'd come again,' he said.

Stevens shrugged his shoulders. 'I trust you won't give my visit any sort of occult meaning,' he said in a cynical tone. 'After all, even though you've been rather rude to me, you're the only civilised person here. I don't like leaving you like this. May I ask where you're going?'

'You may ask. But I can't tell you... You have changed. You are no longer a lost sheep.'

'New clothes,' Lawless went on, in the teasing voice of a nagging woman, as he looked at Stevens' watch chain. 'New clothes, smartly cut. And that indescribable air of the man of property. You have done well, sir. You told me your father was a serf of some sort.' Lawless laughed. His laugh was a sort of cackle.

'Yes,' said Stevens. 'Have your joke. Why not?'

'No, no,' said Lawless in a serious voice. 'It's not a joke. You have done remarkably well. You've been away, I hear.'

Stevens burst into a loud laugh. He took off his hat. His hair was glossy, brushed and scented. He looked dandy, well-groomed and sure of himself. Beside him, the uncouth, bearded figure of Lawless appeared barbaric and degraded.

'So?' said Lawless.

'Yes,' said Stevens, 'you are a humbug. Funny thing, in the yard outside, when I saw the people pinching your kit, I pitied you for a moment. I thought you had really fallen in love with the woman. But of course... I was mistaken. What idea are you amusing yourself with now?'

'Where have you been?' said Lawless.

'Shall I tell you?' said Stevens, going to the window sill. He brushed the window sill with his handkerchief and leaned against it. He crossed his arms on his chest. He wore a brilliant ring on his right hand. Lawless fixed his eyes on the ring.

'Well?' said Lawless dreamily, watching the ring.

Stevens shrugged his shoulders. 'I have become rich.'

'Those lozenges?'

'Yes.' Stevens laughed again. 'For a mystic you have a remarkably acute mind. Yes. I have marketed my lozenge. I think I told you I was going to discover a new god? Don't you envy me?'

Lawless shook his head and looked at the hearth. Suddenly he stopped, picked up some ashes between his fingers and let them drop slowly. 'There. A burnt fire. That's all it leaves. Ashes.'

'Macanasa asked me to come to see you. But I intended coming anyway before I went away. I knew she'd leave you.'

'Why do you always refer to her?' said Lawless quietly. 'Are you going to pursue her – now that you are rich? What is this lozenge of yours?'

'Yes,' said Stevens, 'I knew she'd leave you. I think I managed that very well. You know I'm a sentimentalist. I was once in love. That's why. I hate to see any man injure a woman, though I despise women. When a man is an atheist he has to seek refuge in sentimentality of some sort to... er... save himself from absolute despair. It's only the religious fanatic who can afford to be cruel to women. Like you. I wonder what you would have done to her? Eh? What are you going to do to her husband?'

'Tell me about your lozenge.'

'Yes. I'm a sentimentalist,' continued Stevens. 'I'm willing to take you along with me.'

'Where?' asked Lawless, sitting erect on his stool.

'Wherever you like. In Ireland the people are too primitive for anything like that. Primitive people are too wise. They feel their youth. Youth is ridiculous. It's only when people get old —'

'What are you drivelling about?' said Lawless angrily. 'Has your new wealth driven you mad?'

'Mad!' said Stevens. 'I like that. No. I was offering you a chance to market your discovery. Indeed you might very well make a pot of money out of it.'

Lawless looked at him with contempt. Stevens flinched and broke into a laugh.

'A serf,' said Lawless.

'Yes?'

'You said you managed it all right,' continued Lawless bitterly. He nodded his head several times. 'However...' He sighed. 'You have failed. I am free of you. What is your lozenge? Won't you tell me?'

'I can't tell you. You see, it's not yet for sale. I've sold it to an American syndicate. But it may be something very important. It's certainly bound to be a commercial success. If it does not ensure immortality it ensures possession of amorous powers while life lasts.'

'I see,' said Lawless, clapping his hands together. 'And you... you've done this. That's splendid.'

'Thanks for your congratulations.'

Lawless shook his head. 'I'm not congratulating you,' he said excitedly. 'But this is a sign.'

'Now, now, for goodness sake, don't fly off at a tangent. Remember, at least, that I have some intelligence left, even though I have prostituted my intellect to the gratification of old men's lust. Let's not talk of signs.'

'I don't blame you,' said Lawless. 'But.... it seems to me splendid that this should happen here, where I came to prepare myself. I get an actual glimpse of this corruption to which man clings, calling it life and thinking it beautiful. You see I have cast away everything.'

'So I see.'

'Before you came I felt weak. I have stopped eating. And I thought it was because I lacked the resolution to... Now I see that I needed......'

'Do you know I'm grateful to you in one way,' said Stevens.

Lawless opened his mouth. Then he smiled affectionately. 'Have I...' he began eagerly and then stopped.

'If you hadn't come here I'd probably have spent the rest of my life here... aimlessly.'

Lawless drew back and closed his mouth.

'Fact,' said Stevens. 'Your, what shall I call it, influence roused my ambition again. Not my ambition but my lust of life. I gradually came to realise the idiocy of my gesture of contempt for humanity. If humanity is contemptible then so am I. You with your doctrine of universal love, with its contradictory doctrine of the glorification of the individual, seemed to me so like.... now I'm rambling off.'

'Why try to defend yourself. You feel a culprit going away. But there is no longer need for explanation. How long have I been here?... Time... what is time?... Why are we talking like this?... You don't believe I'm going to do it?'

'Do what?'

'Perhaps if you did believe I wouldn't do it. Perhaps if all believed then nobody would strive, then all would wallow in the corruption that you are now going to encourage and make your god. That's why it's splendid that I found you here and that you are going away. I was abroad once. Even now I can realise the pleasure of it. One must have done that to appreciate its opposite. Once I was drunk for a week and it was very pleasant. No reserve now. For I am going to do it. See. Not one single thing holds me back.' He snapped his fingers.

Stevens stood erect and approached the hearth. 'Say, old man,' he said in a friendly voice. 'You had better come with me.'

Lawless shook his head resolutely.

'Chance brought us here together,' continued Stevens softly and sadly. 'And the same chance mates in nature species that are mutually satisfying. Can't you see that my despair is the complement of your fanatical enthusiasm? And beyond us the herd moves with its myriad mouths browsing on the rich earth. It doesn't heed us. Ours is the brain of the leering god that stings the herd or tends it for our amusement.'

'Oh! This is wearisome,' said Lawless. 'You may wear a rock with dropping water but you can't break it with a straw. Don't use philosophy against my resolution.' He looked up wildly and cried: 'I am going to gamble for a prize that is immeasurable. I tell you now calmly with my other self. See. I see that self, that is going out and up, sitting apart, a rock. I, the fool, the other man like you, tell you that he the other I, shall be God. Because he wills it.'

'Good,' said Stevens sadly. 'I understand you now.'

Lawless furrowed his forehead and trembled, so that he appeared to be on the verge of fainting. Then he shrugged himself and became motionless.

'You are right,' continued Stevens, 'but so am I. Although perhaps you would fill my role better and I yours.'

Stevens leaned against the wall and looked at Lawless with unseeing eyes. He spoke like a poet reciting verses: 'Would it not be fine if I could be the material of godliness, the soft rain that is carried on the wind at will, the dew that sparkles on the grass blade in the morning. Soft, gentle love, the tender heart of love, the ecstasy of the artist swooning in his dreams of beauty. Would that that were God! But it seems that it must be only the handmaid of the Lord, to be whored at will and then spat upon. For God has the cruel eye of an eagle and the voice of the thunderbolt and the uncouth figure of a conqueror, with blood dripping from his sword.'

Lawless was not listening. Stevens stopped, sighed and then looked at Lawless alertly. Lawless was looking out the window. His eyes blinked rapidly and his lips moved. He was becoming exhausted by the effort to contemplate reality while talking to Stevens. His mind was again filling with visions and his body was on guard again, protecting the being that was already kicking in the womb about to burst forth.

'You won't come,' said Stevens softly.

Lawless looked at him, shook his head and then again looked out the window, listening.

'I see,' said Stevens. 'You are afraid of him. Could I do anything? Can't you tell me your plans?'

'Who?' said Lawless, looking at Stevens furtively. 'Who should I fear?'

'Dillon.'

Lawless laughed strangely. 'No, no. I'm not afraid of him. He is my only brother. But he might delay me. I should be gone before he comes. At all costs I must leave him behind.'

'I think I had better go, though I hate leaving you like this. Are you sure I could do nothing? You wouldn't tell me where you are going.'

Suddenly Lawless changed his attitude again and said cunningly: 'Are you quite sure this lozenge of yours is going to be a success?'

'I am positive.'

'Splendid,' said Lawless. 'Europe is doomed. Again beauty will come into its own. People will respond to the voice of beauty. The wordless voice of God.'

Stevens sighed. 'Will you shake hands with me before I go? And forgive me if I have in any way interfered with your plans, whatever they are. If I have offended you, well I am......'

Lawless suddenly threw back his head, looked at Stevens sideways arrogantly and said: 'You couldn't interfere with my plans.'

'Will you shake hands?'

'No,' Lawless smiled suddenly. His right eye gleamed cunningly: 'But I'll bless you if you like.'

Stevens shook his head: 'You are being insincere again.'

'Ha!' cried Lawless. 'See how my contempt for this frothy bubble that you mistake for life gives me the advantage over you. I am triumphant even though I stamp upon it. In another few hours I shall be no more as you know me as a man, and yet, although I am about to make this gesture of defiance, I am triumphant and you doubt, doubt, doubt. You are unhappy.' He laughed quietly and folded his arms.

'All right. I had better leave you.' Stevens walked away. Lawless called after him. Stevens turned about. Lawless said: 'I'll give you a name for your lozenge.'

Stevens responded angrily. 'I don't want a name. You can have your triumph. Mine will last longer than yours... after your death.'

Lawless jumped to his feet. 'You lie,' he shouted.

'No, I don't lie,' said Stevens coldly. 'I came here to see you in pity, because you are a fellow man, and it is perhaps the curse of the atheist that he sincerely pities his fellow man because he pities himself. He pities his manhood which is doomed to die. So I pity you still. But you are unworthy of pity. It is our duty to crush you. Not for the evil you cause yourself, for that is but slight; but for the evil that comes after you, after your death. When fanatics worship your bones and wage wars over your mythical tombs. That won't be your triumph, though, for nature will have swallowed you back into her womb and will smile at man as before, jeering at his vain efforts to unravel her secrets.'

Again Lawless shouted hoarsely: 'And again I say you lie.'

'I am indifferent,' said Stevens, 'whether I lie or do not lie. I am only a cog in a wheel. Or rather a bee in a hive. It does not matter what I think of what any man thinks. What matters is the accumulation of man's knowledge, the increase of his power, the lessening of his suffering. What is good is the submission of the individual to this universal need of man to learn more and more, so that some day man will be so strong that nature will bow before him. What is evil is that some men like you become ashamed of their common manhood. They become ashamed through fear and vanity. And they want to raise themselves above their fellows and become gods. It has always been so. Suffering, laceration, mysticism, murder and war are the wonderful signs of this wonderful divinity. I say it's a cursed cheat. Humbug! Go to your death. I wash my hands of you. I won't raise a finger to prevent your death.'

'Again I say you lie,' shouted Lawless furiously.

'What of it?' Stevens shrugged his shoulders. 'If you know I lie then pardon me and leave me to my flesh-pots.' He turned to the door, stopped and walked out.

'I say,' said Lawless. 'One word.' Stevens came to the doorway and looked in. Lawless had become calm again. Some new current of feeling was bubbling up in him, for he was smiling and rubbing his chin as if thinking of something very humorous. 'When are you going?'

'Tomorrow,' said Stevens.

'Would you do me a favour?'

'What is it?'

'Go now. At once.'

'Why?'

'I mean it for your good. You are, after all, worth more than the others. I know what is going to happen. As you are going back to the flesh-pots I don't want to spoil your progress. If you stay you may get into trouble, as you've been concerned in this. You've been known to come here.' Still smiling, he came forward and put his hand on Stevens's right shoulder. 'Why should you get yourself into trouble?'

'What the devil do you mean? What do you intend to do? Do you mean that you ... ?'

'Now go, I tell you,' said Lawless, still smiling mysteriously. 'Or do you want to sacrifice yourself to save a fellowman? This atheistic pity of yours may indeed be genuine. And yet, because you have been kind to me in your foolish way, I tell you to go.'

'You have some devilish scheme,' murmured Stevens.

Lawless became serious. His face grew sombre and arrogant. 'You wash your hands of me. Go your way.

Save me, would you, with your fine phrases and your smug humanity? Your elaborate reasonings. Your civilisation built on the sweat of slaves. Begone, worm. Philistine. Drug yourself with senile hypocrisy and loll over your flesh-pots while the emasculated slaves rub your loins with ointments. I shall rock the world to its core, shake out its bowels and drench its fragments in a shower of blood. By my will,' he cried, grinding out the words so intently that the veins swelled in his neck. 'By my imperishable will to do it or sacrifice myself.'

Then he clutched Stevens by the shoulder with great force, wrinkled his nostrils and whispered fiercely: 'You who humble yourself before man, do you want to sacrifice yourself for man, to prevent me do this?'

Stevens remained silent. His eyelids lowered and his lips quivered. Then he unloosed Lawless's hold on his shoulder and took a pace backwards. 'I won't interfere with you. Set your mind at rest. I'll go immediately. I won't even warn the police. You are not worth it.' Stevens bowed slightly and moved away a few paces.

'Now,' Lawless cried after him, 'the decks are cleared for action. Science has broken her puny javelin on the rock of my belief. I stand defiant and free. Unconquerable.'

Stevens looked back. Lawless was standing in the doorway with his arms folded, rigid, like a statue. Stevens watched him. Then he looked at the sky and round about. He smiled sadly. He looked at the ground, brooding. He looked up suddenly at Lawless. His face was animated with boyish glee.

'Suppose you are right. Wouldn't that be splendid? Look at the sky. We're going to have a storm. Thunder and lightning to accompany the birth of a new God.' He laughed aloud and walked to the gate. There he paused again. 'No, I won't interfere. When gods are born wise men hide in caves or perhaps, better still, beneath some woman's bed. I won't interfere. But... could you tell when it's going to happen?'

Lawless said nothing.

'Very well,' said Stevens, moving away. 'I'll keep a watch on all the newspapers. This is sure to be a scoop.' Then he coughed and walked away without looking back.

After he had gone some distance, he halted and tried to turn back and struggled with himself. But he went on, wrapt in thought and murmuring to himself: 'There is something sacred in his mania.'

He crossed the river going towards his house. As he mounted the slope, other thoughts entered his mind, thoughts of pleasure, of cities, of women, of riches, of wise conversation. He felt that it was good to be alive. As he ascended the slope life grew more and more magnificent. Every moment became a gem.

CHAPTER XXII

At noon the sky grew dark. The sun disappeared. Shadows moved along the mountain sides. In the glen there was a sultry heat. It was difficult to breathe. Birds ceased to sing. Sounds became strange. The water of the river, flowing slowly, seemed to have an ominous sound.

The people were gathering hay. In the excitement of the morning they had forgotten it and the signs of the coming storm. But as soon as they had taken home what they had snatched from Lawless they rushed into their fields.

All over the glen the people worked in silence, feverishly gathering their hay and carting it homewards. They perspired working. They did not think. They no longer remembered Lawless, nor Dillon, who had lost his wife and children. Now there was labour for their hands and the hard earth to trample under foot and the angry sky above threatening thunderbolts. In their struggle for mastery over nature the evil human thought flowed out through their pores in sweat. Their toil transcended fear and passion and love. Their eyes were fixed on the earth. Their hands grasped the fruits of the earth. They looked neither hither or thither.

When Stevens had gone, Lawless remained in the doorway brooding. His mind was calm. Occasionally he thought 'When?' But his mind was sleepy and it gave no reply to this question. At last he began to walk around the house slowly, with his eyes on the ground and his hands clasped behind his back. Then at one point, when he halted and asked himself the question, he saw the Deegans working in a field towards which his eyes were turned. They were gathering their hay. The grandparents, the parents, the children and even the infant boy were there working. Lawless watched them with interest, without knowing what they were doing or why they were doing it. Deegan was carting the hay. His wife and elder children were loading the cart. The old people were helping as best they could. The little infant boy walked beside his grandfather, carrying wisps of hay to a little pile he was making. The old grandfather gathered the hay with his walking stick because he was unable to stoop much. He continually looked at the sky and made signs with his hands to the others.

Seeing the old man look at the sky, Lawless looked up. He suddenly became wide awake and nervous. The sky was getting very dark. He looked about him furtively, and began to walk up and down in front of the house with his arms crossed on his chest. Curiously, his mind was still sleepy and calm. It was only his body that was excited and nervous. His body watched the increasing darkness and listened suspiciously to the absence of sound. His mind was merely aware that his body was fretfully watching the approaching darkness and listening to the absence of sound. This contradiction in his being became gradually terrifying to him, until at last he halted and cried out:

'Who comes now?'

It was really a human sound that he had heard. Although normally the sound was too dim to be capable of reaching a human ear intact, his senses had now become so sharpened that he heard the sound distinctly.

He looked to the left as soon as he had cried out and saw Macanasa approaching – in the far distance. He was coming down the mountain side from the roadway. Macanasa, as was customary with him, had cut at a gorse bush with his stick. The swishing sound reached Lawless's ears.

Seeing Macanasa approach, Lawless went indoors hurriedly. Now he became aware that it was just as unpleasant and dangerous to be within the house as it was recently to be without the house. He came out again into the yard and wished to turn in some direction away from the approaching old man. But he said aloud: 'I have not yet decided.'

So he retreated again to the doorway and stood there watching. He watched the people work. A vision of universal work entered his mind. He saw all men working, spinning dry grass into a lengthy rope. They circled the earth with the rope and then, winding like a snake, its end dangled into space and fell downwards. The people crawled off the earth down the rope. They all went. He was left alone on the earth.

His mind dreamt on calmly and it seemed to him that it was good to be alone on the earth and that he need strive no more nor go whither he intended going. But as he meditated on this, the old man reached the gate and addressed him. He didn't understand what the old man said, but he heard the words and stepped in from the doorway. 'Begone,' he said angrily. 'Did I not pay you to leave me alone?'

'What's that?' Macanasa pretended not to have heard, although he had heard very well. He entered the yard and approached the house with his hand to his ears, calling out: 'What's that ye said, Mr. Lawless? Is it sick again ye said ye were?'

Lawless did not answer him. Instead he shut the door lest the old man might enter. Then he came to the window and looked out. Macanasa saluted him by touching his hat.

'What do you want now?' said Lawless angrily. 'Have I not given everything away? Do you want my clothes, too?'

'Savin' yer presence,' said Macanasa, 'an' is it yer clothes ye want to strip off an' you goin' to walk the high road?'

The old man came close to the window and touched the frame with his hand. 'The wood is rotten,' he said in an undertone. ' 'Twill cost a power o' money to make the place fit an' comfortable again.'

Then he looked up at Lawless shrewdly. Lawless sniffed and smelt the old man. There was a strong, stale smell of dried perspiration, decaying clothes and tobacco. It seemed peculiarly offensive to Lawless and he felt sure it was the devil's smell. He started violently, and looked behind him furtively for something with which to strike Macanasa.

'A spear,' he said, half aloud.

'A spear,' Macanasa eyed him cautiously. 'Sure a spear wouldn't be any great addition to ye an' you goin' to walk the roads. But if it's a good strong ash plant ye want I'll get one for ye. It's great company for a long journey. They say that St. Patrick carried one.'

'What brought you here, you devil?' shouted Lawless.

'Now that's not a proper way to talk to a man that's wearing himself out to protect ye,' said Macanasa in a confidential manner. 'Yes, to protect ye an' send ye on a safe journey, free from knives an' ropes. Aye, ropes. Ropes.'

'What ropes?'

'Well, then, a rope,' said Macanasa, 'although he may have more than one for all I know.'

'Who?'

'Dillon,' whispered Macanasa. 'But don't start. I sent him off. Only for a little while, though.'

'Why did you send him off?'

'Just because,' said Macanasa mysteriously. 'The storm'll soon be on us,' he added after a pause. 'It may last for days. This place is awful in a storm. Trees do fall on the house and the river flooded that high, so yer thigh's 'd be wetted walkin' on high stones. Aye! A dangerous ruffian of a place. If I had my choice it's out of it I'd tramp before I'd be an hour nearer the grave.'

'Where did he go to?' said Lawless.

'He went down to the priest's house,' said Macanasa in a whisper. 'The priest might be comin' shortly. He's a hard man in a temper. It's best to keep out of his way an' he in a temper. I wouldn't care to be in this house when he comes, not for the finest two-year-old that was ever bred.'

'I can't go while you're here.'

'Sure it's not askin' ye to go I am. Only I have to look after the place for fear of poachin' neighbours when yer gone.'

'At dawn,' said Lawless in an undertone.

'At dawn, did ye say?' said Macanasa.

'Yes,' said Lawless in a loud voice. 'At dawn. I have decided now. I see it clearly.'

'An' ye'll be the night here then?'

Lawless nodded.

'Would I stay the night with ye for company?'

Lawless laughed and leaned out of the window. 'Ah! It would be perhaps splendid to get you too in my grasp when the moment comes and my power is unfurled like the banner of an army. What! A flood!'

There was a long pause. Lawless was leaning out of the window, looking, not at Macanasa, but at the labourers in the hayfield. Macanasa, with a raven's eyes, watched Lawless. Then Lawless said softly:

'What are they doing there?'

Macanasa made no answer. Lawless turned on him angrily and cried: 'What are they doing there?'

Macanasa stepped back, took off his hat and said cunningly: 'God protect ye from the evil one. I see nobody.'

Then Lawless laughed aloud. He pointed his finger at Macanasa and said jeeringly: 'Ha! You fool! You think you can delude a crazy man even now with your cunning. Bah! I have now attained all attributes. Even the cunning of the damned. Fool! Go, gather you weeds, for tomorrow the lily is in flower and none to pluck with me the fruits of my toil. The swine are rooting for acorns while the golden fruit is hanging ripe in the heavens and ready to fall with the first rays of dawn.'

'And suppose,' began Macanasa in a whisper.

He said no more. Lawless watched him, listening.

'Suppose he comes back with the rope,' said Macanasa angrily.

'Listen!'

'Yes, yer honour,'

'I have made a bargain with you.'

'Yes, yer honour.'

'On condition that you do not come near this house before noon tomorrow.'

'Why so, yer honour?'

'If you come I'll know. Even at a distance. In that case I'll –'

'You'll what, yer honour?'

Lawless stared at him intently. Then Macanasa gravely nodded his head. Lawless also nodded his head.

'I'll go now,' said Macanasa, 'an' if he comes—'

'If he comes, we shall both go.'

'Together?'

'Perhaps together. Perhaps in opposite directions.'

Macanasa paused. Then Lawless again became angry and shouted:

'Why don't you go?'

'I'm gone,' cried Macanasa, darting backwards. 'And the horned devil couldn't bring me nearer this cursed house again till yer out of it.'

'Good,' said Lawless. 'Until noon.'

He waited until Macanasa had disappeared. Then he came out of the house and watched the old man until he had crossed the river. He went into the house again and left the door wide open.

CHAPTER XXIII

Then indeed his mind became possessed by visions of such strange quality that he completely lost his reason and stood in the middle of the room, incapable of movement. Around him, space became full of tormenting spirits. The walls of the room grew to an enormous size and became inscribed with obscene mottoes, which were continually changing shape and colour. Many gods were there among the tormenting spirits. Each god screamed in a different language. Each carried different instruments of torture. They held in their formless hands animals and birds representative of their power and ferocity, snakes, eagles, leopards, lions and weasels. One carried on a golden string a falcon with flaming spurs. Another had an elephant's trunk protruding from his forehead. Their alien faces were distorted with anger. They foamed at the mouth and their hoary beards floated on their breasts, with a black claw attached to each hair, jingling as they floated. Their words came out in flames, curled on the air like smoke and then were caught by attendant spirits and carried to the walls, where they were translated into pictures.

There was a turmoil as of a great battle from this contention of the shouting gods and their vassals. And his soul, the object of their frenzy, crouched within his being, rushing hither and thither, also screaming, and begging for mercy. It appealed to each god in turn but in vain, for each appeal was answered by a derisive shout, the roar of a lion, the cry of an eagle, the trumpeting of an elephant.

Then they all vanished in a pale flame. There was a pause and then a crash shook the house. He threw himself on the floor and covered his head with his hands. The storm had come. The first peal of thunder rumbled through the sky and died away, reverberating through the mountain glens. Then softly, softly, rain fell in a gentle shower through the heated air, wearily falling to the earth. He opened his eyes, raised his head and began to pray aloud: 'Oh! My soul, I go wherever you desire. I dare all things for your immortal beauty. Give me strength to endure to the end and then go unconquered from darkness to eternal light. Unborn being within the womb of my being, the hour of your birth is approaching.'

Then he arose from the ground and groped about for his stool. Night was falling now. It was dark in the room, except when a flash of lightning illuminated it. He found the stool and sat down. He was trembling but he was no longer afraid. He felt excited and he listened attentively, waiting to hear some message from within himself.

Instead he heard a voice outside the house. 'Are ye there, Mr. Lawless?'

He was not surprised at hearing the voice. He recognised it at once, but made no answer. He looked about him and held out his hand, pointing to the wall opposite the window. 'We shall both sit here by the wall, and watch the lightning flash through the window.'

'Mr. Lawless, are ye there?'

'Yes. I am here,' said Lawless.

Dillon entered the room. He wore a shabby overcoat. He was drenched with rain, and as he walked across the room his boots squelched. He stood near Lawless. Neither spoke for a few moments. Then Lawless said: 'There is only one seat.'

'I don't want a seat,' said Dillon. 'I didn't come on a visit. '

'Why did you come, then?'

'I'm tired all the same. It doesn't matter to me where I sit. '

'Sit by the wall, opposite the window. There is more light.'

'Why should I sit there?'

'See. I'll sit beside you. So we may both be equal. Then you have nothing to fear. Nor have I.'

Lawless got up, touched Dillon gently on the arm and then sat down by the wall. Dillon did not move.

'Maybe it's not worth my while to sit down after all,' he said in a tired, harsh voice.

Lawless said nothing. Again there was a long silence. Lawless spoke in a loud, angry voice: 'Why don't you speak?'

'I'll bide my time,' said Dillon in the same tired, harsh voice. 'Maybe I will and maybe I won't.'

'Won't what?' shouted Lawless. 'This is not the time to play with me, my man. I'm past all that now.'

'I'm not your man, Mr. Lawless.' Now Dillon's voice was bitter and aggressive. 'I've no master.'

Lawless lowered his voice and said: 'Sit down beside me.'

'Very well, then. Maybe it's best to talk sittin' down.' He sat down and stretched out his legs. Then he sighed several times in succession. Neither of them could see the other, although their shoulders touched as they breathed. The air was still very sultry. In spite of the thunder, the lightning and the falling weary rain it was very still there; so still and remote that they became subdued. They sat silently, side by side, and for a long time neither thought nor felt.

At last Dillon spoke slowly, without emotion, as if he were thinking aloud of something trivial and remote. 'I didn't go to the priest, as I was bid. For what is a priest to me now? – no more than last year's rain.'

'Yes, brother,' whispered Lawless. 'Priests are no more than symbols of dead gods. Dry dust scattered by the wind.'

'What could he do for me? What can any man do for me? Fitter to die than to live when a man is left alone on his hearth without the voices of them he fondled.'

'You accuse me?' said Lawless clutching Dillon's arm. 'Man, you accuse me?'

Dillon raised his voice and said querulously: 'Why shouldn't you suffer for it as well as me? And more than me? That's why I came back here without goin' to the priest. I never in all my life took my revenge or the law into me hands, same as any man. But I knew ye wouldn't be gone, because yer conscience 'd be troublin' ye.'

'What have I done to you?'

'You've taken me children.'

'This is indeed human gratitude. I have given my whole life, my wealth and my genius to them and they accuse me of theft.'

'I don't care what you gave. I had never any wealth to give. But whatever time I could I gave bread to the poor. I never injured no man or beast, either. And God Almighty be my witness 'twas little comfort I had in me life except them two little ones. Now they're gone. She took 'em away. Maybe another man would take the law of her. But it's cruelty to part a child from its mother. Little Johnny and Louisa. I think I was fonder of Louisa.

She fell outa the cradle on to the flag in front of the hearth and there's a little mark there yet over her eye. The right eye it is. Did ye ever have a child?'

He began to wander in his mind. He continued to speak without waiting for an answer. Lawless was becoming very excited. He kept moving away from Dillon by making slight movements at intervals with various parts of his body.

'Oh! Lord God!' said Dillon. 'Why is everything so queer? One day the sun is shinin' and ye get a lump in yer throat lookin' at the flowers and listenin' to the birds singin' or maybe watchin' the fish sportin' in the river, and then next day there is black dirty rain an' ye can hear the mud o' the earth sighin' with misery. That's how it is. These years I've been thinkin' of it. An' indeed she was no comfort to me, although I loved her. But they were a comfort to me, and when I used to dandle them on my knee an' I singin' little songs to them with nobody else in the house, I was livin' in a world all o' me own, with nobody to point a finger at me. An' always when I was alone, maybe living on the river bank or ploughing in the field with the sun shinin' on the black earth all round me and the horse swingin' his tail an' me all sleepy with the smell of wet clay, then the world was always full of angels an' no man injured another. And maybe 'twill be that way yet when everybody is a labourer. But I'll be gone then an' I'll never see them again, either. Maybe it would be better not to see them. But all the same—'

Then he started and peered towards Lawless in the darkness. Lawless had managed to move away a little while he had been speaking.

'Ye can't get away,' shouted Dillon, angrily.

'Where should I go?' said Lawless in a weak voice.

'None o' yer dodges,' growled Dillon, 'I've a score to settle with ye.'

'What do you intend to do?' whispered Lawless.

'Yer number's up,' said Dillon harshly. 'Bloody skunks like you haven't the courage of a mouse. I'll give you a fair chance though.'

'You mean to kill me?' gasped Lawless.

Dillon did not reply. Then Lawless laughed harshly.

'Eh?' shouted Dillon in a terrified voice. 'What are ye laughin' at me like that for? Ye can't laugh at me. I'll let no man laugh at me. Least of all you. What devil's tricks are ye up to now?'

There was silence. Then Lawless laughed again, a demented laugh. Then again there was silence. Then Lawless said in a mocking voice:

'So this is how I end. All my dreams.... in a lonely hut... by the hand of a boor. Not even... I cannot raise my hand.' Then he shouted defiantly: 'Strike, you fool. What have you got – a knife?'

'You be quiet now,' said Dillon harshly. 'Maybe you'll have to suffer a little yet. But if you laugh again I'll drive it into ye in the dark. I have two knives, though. You can have one if ye want to fight.' He paused, and then he said, mockingly: 'But I know you won't fight, damn ye. So I'll have to... I can't use a knife on meself.'

'Mock now, you devils,' said Lawless in a low voice.

They both became silent. The storm was now very violent. Lightning flashed repeatedly and the rain pattered heavily on the roof. But the loudest sound within the room was the dripping of water to the hearthstone from a crack in the roof. Tip, tap, it said. And it was louder in the room than the thunder claps.

Both men listened to it. Their strange anger became exhausted again. Dillon began to mutter disjointedly about the children. Then Lawless cried out mournfully: 'I can't resist. I don't know. I must accept. If I could even hate you then I would have strength to fight. Brother, when you have killed me what do you mean to do?'

'I'm going.... I can't say. You might be up to some trick.'

'He suspects me even now. Come, come. It cannot be so dark. Could I not...'

'What's that?' said Dillon, suspiciously. Lawless sat up stiff against the wall, gazed out the window and made his body rigid. 'Come now,' he cried in a loud voice.

'Who are ye callin' to?' shouted Dillon, getting on to his hands and knees and peering out the window. 'Who's outside?'

'Up, up,' cried Lawless, in an exalted voice. 'I am still unconquered. Come, slaves, from your tombs. Throw away the shackles of death. Arise with me.'

'Stop that, ye devil,' gasped Dillon becoming terrified.

'Lo! From the womb comes the spirit of revolt. Listen to the stamping feet of millions. Fly now, wild birds, among the high peaks, floating with slowly flapping heavy wings, over deep voids among the whirling stars. Fly where angels sit among the snows on upstanding rocks. Up winding paths, trodden by wild goats, through the heather. Up, up, until the great sea wind comes roaring through the sky, carrying the echoes of tidal waves in far-off lands. Up, up to the towering summit of the earth. Whither yet souls? Through the sea, where the great eels wind among the swaying weeds, round and round the surface of the earth, where the cold icebergs loom through the Arctic fogs, where the flying fish rise before the prows of ships, flutter and fall again, where the loud whale spouts and the porpoise leaps in the sun. Come souls and share this lovely majesty.'

'Sit still,' shouted Dillon, jumping to his feet.

He pulled a knife from the pocket of his overcoat. He opened it. Lawless started when he heard the blade click.

Then he sang again: 'Hearken to my dream, to my vision of a constant beauty. Listen in awe and arise singing, going into strange worlds on wings. Then strange things shall become beautiful. Soon, soon, for the sinner is about to strike.'

He jumped to his feet. As he did so, Dillon uttered a cry and sprang upon him. Lawless gasped. The knife had gashed his shoulder. He reeled against the wall. Dillon struck again.

'Now I've got ye.'

Then he stepped back and dropped the knife to the floor. Lawless grasped the wall. He muttered something and then fell to the floor. He began to groan. Then he became silent. Dillon stood still.

'Strike a light,' moaned Lawless in a faint voice.

'Light,' said Dillon in a whisper.

Again there was silence. Then Dillon began to murmur.

'Light,' gasped Lawless. 'Give me a light. I am alone. There is nothing here. Guide. Guide, I say. What abyss is this?'

Dillon laughed softly. Then he put his hand within his overcoat.

'Ha!' he said aloud.

He spat and rushed out of the house. Lawless uttered a loud cry and tried to rise, but he fell forward on his face. His blood was flowing freely and his strength was almost exhausted. But he kept crawling towards the door inch by inch, muttering:

'Light! Light!'

CHAPTER XXIV

Again the valley became full of gentle sound and radiant with sunlight. Again the earth shimmered like a many-coloured jewel and the river, gorged with a great flood, flowed thundering, adorned with golden foam. Dawn had come. The storm had faded to a fluttering breeze that gently swayed the ripe corn and the fruit upon the hawthorn bushes.

From the branch of a tree in front of the cottage Dillon hung by the neck, supine and still. His head was muffled in the folds of his shabby overcoat.

Opposite him, prone over the threshold of the house, with his hands stretched out as if in a last appeal, Lawless lay.

His dead face looked beautiful and calm.

BY THE SAME AUTHOR

The Black Soul

The sea roars dismally round the shores of Inverara.
A Stranger takes a room on the island. Here lives a couple whose married years have been joyless . . . until the presence of the Stranger unleashes their passions . . . .
For as spring softens the wild beauty of Inverara, the Stranger becomes conscious of the dark-haired Mary – how summer makes her shiver with life. He is the first man she has ever loved, and she thrills with sexual awakening.
But with autumn comes danger. Peasants mutter superstition against Mary; Red John laughs at nothing, there's murder in his eyes; and a madman's yell hurls the Stranger back to sanity . . . .
Intense, compelling, beautifully descriptive –
as *Wuthering Heights* is to the Yorkshire moors,
so *The Black Soul* is to the Aran Islands.

ISBN 0 86327 478 1

Famine

Famine is the story of three generations of the Kilmartin family set in the period of the Great Famine of the 1840s. It is a masterly historical novel, rich in language, character and plot, a panoramic story of passion, tragedy and resilience.
'The author's skill as a storyteller is at times breathtaking. This is a most rewarding novel.' ***Publishers Weekly***
'I gladly accept one of the claims on the dustjacket of this novel:"A major achievement – a masterpiece,".... it is the kind of truth only a major writer of fiction is capable of portraying.'
Anthony Burgess, Irish Press

ISBN 0 86327 043 3

Short Stories

The Pedlar's Revenge

'This valuable collection displays O'Flaherty's amazing range from a love idyll between a wild drake and a domestic duck to the unspeakable comedy of the appalling Patsa delivering the contents of his golden belly under the influence of a cataclysmic purge, from the burning of young love in that splendid story "The Caress", to the rheumy old man sitting by the roadside and failing to recognise in the old woman, who pauses in passing, the warm love of his youth.' ***Benedict Kiely***

'... a gallery of human emotions, embracing a clutch of huge eccentrics, sweet and sour remembrances of distant youth and vivid portraits of rural Ireland ...'

The Sunday Times

ISBN 0 86327 536 2